CW01064119

Sapper is the pen name of Herm
at the Naval Prison in Bodmin,
Governor. He served in the Roy
as 'sappers') from 1907–19, being awarded the Military Cross
during World War I.

He started writing in France, adopting a pen name because
serving officers were not allowed to write under their own
names. When his first stories, about life in the trenches, were
published in 1919, they were an enormous success. But it was his
first thriller, *Bulldog Drummond* (1920), that launched him as
one of the most popular novelists of his generation. It had several
amazingly successful sequels, including *The Black Gang*, *The
Third Round* and *The Final Count*. Another great success was
Jim Maitland (1923), featuring a footloose English sahib in
foreign lands.

Sapper published nearly thirty books in total, and a vast
public mourned his death when he died in 1937, at the early age
of forty-eight. So popular was his 'Bulldog Drummond' series
that his friend, the late Gerard Fairlie, wrote several Bulldog
Drummond stories after his death under the same pen name.

ASK FOR RONALD STANDISH
THE BLACK GANG
BULLDOG DRUMMOND
BULLDOG DRUMMOND AT BAY
CHALLENGE
THE DINNER CLUB
THE FEMALE OF THE SPECIES
THE FINAL COUNT
THE FINGER OF FATE
THE ISLAND OF TERROR
JIM BRENT
JOHN WALTERS
KNOCK-OUT
MUFTI
THE RETURN OF BULLDOG DRUMMOND
SERGEANT MICHAEL CASSIDY RE
TEMPLE TOWER
THE THIRD ROUND

SAPPER

JIM MAITLAND

HOUSE OF
STRATUS

This edition published in 2008 by House of Stratus, an imprint of
Stratus Books Ltd., 21 Beeching Park, Kelly Bray,
Cornwall, PL17 8QS, UK.

www.houseofstratus.com

A catalogue record for this book is available from the British Library
and the Library of Congress.

ISBN 07551-168-0-1

CONTENTS

FOREWORD

The first time I heard Jim Maitland's name mentioned was two days out of Colombo, going East; and when I confessed my complete ignorance of the man a sort of stupefied silence settled on the company.

"You don't know Jim?" murmured an Assam tea-planter. "I thought everyone knew Jim."

"Anyway, if you stay in these parts long you soon will," put in someone else. "And once known – never forgotten."

Later I asked the tea-planter point-blank for further details.

He smiled thoughtfully.

"Ever been in a brawl, Leyton, with ten men up against you? Well, that's Jim's idea of heaven, though he'd prefer it to be twenty. Have you ever seen a man shoot the pip out of the ace of diamonds at ten paces? Jim cuts it out by shooting round it at twenty. He's long and thin, and he wears an eyeglass. Rumour has it that once some man laughed at that eyeglass." The tea-planter grinned. "Take my advice and don't. It's not safe. He never forgives and he never forgets – but he'd sell the shirt off his back to help a pal. Who he is and what he is I can't tell you. I've never asked; Jim doesn't encourage curiosity."

"Yes – but what does he *do*?" I asked.

"Do? He lives: he doesn't vegetate as nine out of ten of us have to."

The door closed behind him and for a while I sat on thinking. Nine out of ten! Ninety-nine out of a hundred would have been nearer the mark.

Now, since the doings of the one may be of interest to the ninety and nine, I have ventured to put on record these random recollections. For Fate decreed that I was to meet Jim Maitland, and eat and drink and fight with him as my greatest friend.

CHAPTER 1

Raymond Blair – Drunkard

You probably do not know the Island of Tampico. In many ways you are to be pitied, for if ever there was a flawless jewel set in a sapphire sea Tampico is that jewel; and because flawless jewels are few and far between the loss is yours.

But on balance you win. For if ever there was a place where soul and body rotted more rapidly and more completely I have yet to find it. That beautiful island, a queen even amongst the glories of the South Seas, contained more vice to the square mile than the slums of a great city. For in any city there is always work to be done; but in Tampico there was no work to be done. Since fruit and enough food could be had for the asking, there was no struggle to survive. Only one thing had to be paid for – drink.

It was many hundred miles out of the beaten track of the big liners. Only small boats called, principally engaged in the fruit trade, with passenger accommodation for six in the first class. For fruit was the particular trade of Tampico; fruit and various tropical products which grew so richly to hand that it was almost unnecessary to pick them. If you waited long enough they fell into your hands. Nobody ever did anything but wait in Tampico; that is why it is so utterly rotten.

Even when a lump of ambergris comes ashore the fortunate finder does not hurry. There is a dealer in the town, and ambergris means drink for weeks.

The first time I saw Raymond Blair he had just found a lump, and was utterly happy. I had heard about him from MacAndrew the trader, and I watched him with the pitiful interest a sound man always feels for the down and out.

"The most hopeless case of all," MacAndrew had said to me in the club the night before. "A brilliantly educated man – he'll spout classics at you by the yard, and if he's in good form he'll keep a dinner-table in roars of laughter."

"He belongs to the club?" I said in some surprise.

MacAndrew shrugged his shoulders.

"He's got money – quite a bit of money. It comes out every month. And he's educated – a gentleman – and a drunkard. Hopeless, helpless, unredeemable." He filled his pipe thoughtfully. "It's a strange thing to say, but it's better to keep him drunk. It's all that keeps what little manhood is left in him alive. When he's sober he's dreadful.

"Towards the end of the month always, before the money comes – he isn't a man. He will do anything to get drink. There's a Dago here who torments him. He loathes him because one night Blair put it across him in a battle of words, so that the whole club roared with laughter. And the Dago gets his revenge that way. Why, I've seen him, when Blair has been crawling on the floor for the price of a drink, make him stand up on a table and recite 'Humpty Dumpty,' and then give him a few coppers as a reward."

"But can't anything be done?" I asked.

MacAndrew laughed a little sadly.

"When you've been here a little longer, you won't ask that question."

I was sitting in the window of the club as Raymond Blair came in, and we had the room to ourselves. He had been pointed out to me a few days before, but he had then been far too drunk to recognise anybody, and from the look he gave me as he crossed the room it was evident that he regarded me as a stranger. I took no notice of him, and after a while he came over and drew up a chair.

"A stranger, I think, sir, to our island?"

"I arrived about a week ago," I answered a little abruptly. Somehow or other the thought of this English gentleman standing on a table reciting nursery rhymes stuck in my throat.

"And are you staying long?"

"Probably a month," I said. "It depends."

He nodded, and it was then that I saw he was already drunk.

"A charming island," he remarked, and his hand went out to the bell-push. "We must really have a drink to celebrate your first visit."

"Thank you – not for me," I answered briefly.

"As you like," he remarked, with a wave of his hand. "Most new arrivals refuse to drink with me. They hope to save me from myself. But I'm glad to say it's quite useless."

He took a long gulp of what the native waiter had placed beside him without even asking for orders.

"I am only myself now," he continued gravely, "when I am drunk."

It was then, I think, that I realised what an utterly hopeless case he was; but I said nothing and let him ramble on.

"I get my money monthly as a rule." He was gazing dreamily out of the window, across the water to the white line of surf where the lazy Pacific swell lifted and beat on a great coral reef. "This month it has not arrived. Most strange; most peculiar. The boat came in as usual, but nothing for me. And so you can imagine my feelings when I found yesterday afternoon a quite considerable lump of ambergris on the shore. The trouble is that the dealer is such a robber. A scandalous price, sir, he gave me – scandalous, though better than nothing. Still, I am afraid my less fortunate friends outside will have to suffer for his miserliness. Charity and liquor both begin at home. It is the one comfort of having the club: one can escape from them."

I glanced into the street, and there I saw his "friends" – five haggard unshaven human derelicts clustered under the shade of a palm tree, eyeing the door of the club hungrily, wolfishly, waiting for him to share with them some of the proceeds of his find.

"As you see," he continued affably, "they are not quite qualified for election even to the Tampico club." He dismissed the thought of them with a wave of his hand. "Tell me, sir, does the Thames still glint like a silver-grey streak by Chelsea Bridge as the sun goes down? Do the barges still go chugging past Westminster? Do children still sail boats on the Round Pond back London way?"

For the life of me I could not speak. The pathos of it all had me by the throat. Back London way –

With wistful eyes he was staring once more over the wonderful blue of the sea, and he seemed to me as a man who saw visions and dreamed dreams – dreams of the might-have-been; dreams of a dead past. Then he pulled himself together and was himself once more – Raymond Blair, drunkard and derelict.

As for me, the moment of pity had passed; but it left its mark. The memory of the tragedy in his face stuck to me. Maybe it made me more tolerant than others were: more tolerant certainly than Jim Maitland. For it was in Tampico that I first met Jim, and Blair was the unwitting cause of it.

It must have been a month or five weeks later. The fortnightly boat had just come in, and I intended to leave Tampico in her next day. It was tea-time, and as I turned into the club I saw a stranger lounging on the veranda. In the outposts of Empire one does not wait for an introduction, and I went up to him and spoke. He rose, and I noticed that he was very tall.

"I'd better introduce myself," he said with a faint and rather pleasant drawl. "My name is Maitland – Jim Maitland."

I looked at him with suddenly awakened interest. So this was the man of whom the Assam tea-planter had spoken – the celebrated Jim Maitland who lived and didn't vegetate. I can see him now – tall, lean and sinewy, the bronzed clean-cut face tanned with years of outdoor life – and the quite unnecessary eyeglass. Of the real Jim Maitland – of his charm, his incredible lack of fear, his great heart, I knew nothing at the time. That afternoon in Tampico I saw only the outside man, and, in spite of the eyeglass, I pronounced him good.

"Yes, I know most of the odd corners out here," he said. "Though funnily enough I've never been to Tampico before. I've just arrived in the boat, and I want to get off in her again tomorrow, rather particularly."

A peculiar half-amused look came into his eyes for a moment, and then changed, I thought, to sadness. But maybe it was only my imagination.

"You know this place well?" he said.

"I've been here six weeks," I answered. "I'm going tomorrow myself."

"Six weeks should be enough for you to tell me what I want to know. I joined the *Moldavia* at Port Said, and struck up an acquaintance with a little woman on board. She was all by herself – and she was coming here. In fact, she's come this afternoon by the boat to join her husband. I gather he's a fruit merchant in Tampico on rather a big scale. Well, when we berthed there was no sign of him on the landing. So I took her up to that shack of a hotel, and started to make inquiries. I couldn't find out anything, so I came along here."

He rose suddenly.

"Hullo! here she is."

I glanced up and saw a sweet-looking girl coming towards us along the dusty street. It seemed to me as if Tampico had vanished, and I was standing in an old English garden with the lilac in full bloom.

"Mr Leyton," murmured Maitland, and I bowed.

She nodded at me charmingly, and then gave him the sweetest of smiles.

"I couldn't wait in the hotel, Jim," she said. "It's a horrible place."

"The Tampico hotel," I laughed, "is not a hotel, but a sports club for the insect world."

She sat down, and I glanced at Jim Maitland. His eyes were fixed on the girl with that same strange expression in them that I had noticed before – the expression that in years to come I was to see so often.

I realised he was speaking.

"He can't have got your letter, Sheila. Or perhaps he may be away on business."

"Well, I asked everyone at the hotel, after you went out, but they didn't seem to understand."

Maitland turned to me.

"Mrs Blair has lost or mislaid her husband," he remarked whimsically. "A large reward is offered for information."

"Blair?" I said, puzzled. "A fruit merchant? I don't seem to know the name."

"Surely you must know him – Raymond Blair."

For a moment it seemed as if everything turned black. Then –

"How stupid of me," I remarked steadily. "Raymond Blair! Why – of course. The last time I saw him he was going into the interior, and he did say, if I remember right, that he might be catching the boat which left a fortnight ago."

I felt the eye behind that eyeglass boring into me, and I wouldn't meet it. Instead I watched the smile fade from her face, to be replaced by a little pitiful questioning look which she turned on Jim Maitland.

"Perhaps I could go to his house," she said doubtfully. "If you could tell me where it is."

Now I was lying desperately.

"He was going to have it done up," I remarked. "I think, Mrs Blair, that the best thing to do would be for you to go back to the hotel while I make inquiries."

It was at that moment that MacAndrew passed by to go into the club and nodded to me.

"Perhaps your friend might know," she hazarded.

There was nothing for it, and I rose and caught MacAndrew by the arm. My grip was not gentle, and my eyes blazed a message at him.

"Mrs Blair has come out to join her husband, Mac," I said. "You know – Raymond Blair."

I heard him mutter under his breath, but MacAndrew could keep as steady a face as I.

"I have a sort of idea that he sailed on business by the last boat, didn't he?" I continued.

He took his cue.

"I believe he did," he said thoughtfully.

Then Jim Maitland began to take a hand. "I think you had better do what this gentleman suggested, Sheila. I'll take you back to the hotel, and I'll see you get a good room. Then you can lie down and rest for a bit, while we find out for certain."

He turned to us, and we knew he'd guessed something. "Shall I find you here when I've seen Mrs Blair back to the hotel?"

We nodded.

"Where is he, Mac?" I said, when they had gone.

"In Dutch Joe's," he answered. "And they're baiting him. He's got no money. Who is the fellow with the pane of glass in his eye?"

"Jim Maitland," I remarked briefly, and MacAndrew whistled.

"So that's Jim Maitland, is it?" he said slowly. "Well, if one-tenth of the yarns about him are true, there will be murder done tonight."

Five minutes later Jim Maitland strode up to us. "Mrs Blair is a friend of mine. I don't know her husband from Adam, but I know her. You take me?"

His blue eyes, hard as steel, searched our faces.

"Well, gentlemen, I'm waiting. I don't know what the game is, but your lies wouldn't have deceived an unweaned child who knew these parts."

Strangely enough I felt no offence.

"I lied right enough," I said heavily. "I lied for her benefit, not yours."

"Why?" snapped Maitland.

"You'd better come and see for yourself," said MacAndrew.

"Then Raymond Blair is on the island?"

"He is," returned MacAndrew briefly.

In silence he led the way along the dusty street towards the native part of the little town. Once or twice I stole a glance at Jim Maitland's face as he strode along between us, and it was hard and set, almost as if he realised what was in front of him. But he spoke no word during the ten minutes it took us to reach Dutch Joe's; only a single long-drawn "Ah!" came from his lips when he realised our destination.

MacAndrew flung open the door and we stepped inside.

I can see the place now – Dutch Joe leaning over the bar, and a dozen or so Greeks, English, Germans, Chinamen, grinning as they watched Blair cringing before a swarthy-looking Dago sitting at a table by himself.

It was the Dago who noticed us first, and an ugly sneer appeared on his face. Baiting his enemy would prove more interesting in front of three of his own countrymen.

"Thank you, Mr Blair," he remarked affably. "A most excellent imitation. You will now please stand on the table and recite 'Mary had a Little Lamb.' You will then get this nice shining dollar."

I had one brief vision of a man in an unnecessary eyeglass going in on that Dago, and then the fighting began. Blair had subsided foolishly in a corner and was forgotten. In a fight of that sort you scrap with the nearest man whose nationality is not your own. Out of the tail of my eye I saw no less than four fights going on, while Dutch Joe cursed everyone impartially.

It was hot while it lasted, so hot that I had no chance to see what an artist Jim Maitland was till quite the end. Then I saw him do a thing I have never seen before or since. His Dago had gone down twice and was snarling like a mad dog. There was murder in his heart, and there would have been murder in that room if he had been fighting anyone else.

Like a flash of light he flung a knife at Maitland, and I heard afterwards that he could skewer a card to the wall at ten paces five times out of six. It was then that Jim did this thing – so quick that my eye scarce followed it. He side-stepped, and caught the knife in his right hand by the hilt, and flung it back. And the next moment it was quivering in the fleshy part of the right arm of that Dago.

"Get out of it," said Jim tersely; "I'll bring Blair."

Next minute we were out into the sunny street. I was sweating and MacAndrew was breathing hard, but Jim hadn't turned a hair. His face wore a faint satisfied smile.

"Not bad," he remarked quietly. "But it was time to leave. They'll be drawing guns soon."

Even as he spoke, there came the sudden sharp crack of a revolver from Dutch Joe's.

With Jim on one side and me on the other, and MacAndrew pushing behind, we got Raymond Blair along. We took him to MacAndrew's house, and held a council of war.

"What are we going to do?" Jim said. "She thinks he's a prosperous fruit trader. And there he is. Why on earth didn't you say he was dead?" Jim swung round on me, and I shrugged my shoulders.

"It might have been better, I admit," I answered. "But think of the complications."

There was silence in the room while Jim Maitland paced up and down smoking furiously. Suddenly he stopped, and I saw he had come to a decision.

"There's only one thing for it," he said. "His wife must know: it's impossible to keep it from her. If we say he's gone on a voyage, she'll wait here till he comes back. She's got to see him. At his best, you understand? At his best."

He was staring out of the window, and MacAndrew's eyes and mine met.

"Aye, lad," said the gruff Scotchman gently, "it's the only straight game."

He rose and crossed to a cupboard in the corner, took out a bottle and handed it to Blair. Then, signing to us to follow him, he left the room…

Five minutes passed; ten – and then we heard the sounds of footsteps coming along the passage. They were comparatively steady, and Jim, who had been standing motionless staring out of the window, swung slowly round as the door opened and Raymond Blair came in. He was still shaky; his face was still grey and lined, but he was sane. He was a man again.

"I thank you, MacAndrew," he said quietly. "It was badly needed."

Then he realised that there was a stranger present.

"Mr Blair, I believe," remarked Jim in an expressionless voice.

"That is my name," returned the other.

"I have recently arrived from England, Mr Blair," continued Jim, "and your wife was with me on the boat."

Raymond Blair clutched at the table with a little shaking cry.

"She is at the hotel waiting to see her husband, whom she believes to be a prosperous fruit trader."

I couldn't help feeling sorry for him. His distress was too pitiful. Even Jim Maitland's eyes softened a little as we heard how he'd lied to her in his letters, writing glowing accounts of the success of his fictitious business; how on one excuse and another he had prevented her coming out to join him before. We heard, too, that the money each month had not come from any business at home, but from her, out of her small private means. He had pretended he was investing it for her in the island.

Gradually a new note crept into his voice – the note of hope. The reason for the non-arrival of the usual remittance was clear now: she had come – his little Sheila. With her at his side he could make a new start; she would help him to fight against his craving.

Jim's voice broke in, quiet and assured.

"You had better come and see her at the hotel now, Mr Blair. But on one thing I insist. You must tell her what you have told us here tonight, otherwise I shall tell her myself."

That was almost the last I ever saw of Raymond Blair. I saw him go to his wife in the hotel; I saw her welcome him with a glad little cry, though even then it seemed to me that her eyes went over his shoulder to Jim…

An hour later she came down the stairs, and her face made me catch my breath with the pity of it.

"Where is Mr Maitland?" she said quietly, and at that moment he came in.

From then on her eyes never left his face; as far as she was concerned MacAndrew and I were non-existent.

"Why did you give him that bottle of gin?" she asked, still in the same quiet voice. "Why did you send my husband to me drunk just after he had recovered from a dose of fever?"

I saw MacAndrew's jaw drop, but it was Jim Maitland I was staring at. After one sudden start of pure amazement, he gave no sign; he just stood there quietly, looking at her with thoughtful eyes.

11

"I trusted you utterly," she went on. "You were good to me on the boat and I thought you were my friend. Oh, how dared you do such a wicked, wicked thing?"

I opened my mouth to speak, but Jim Maitland's hand gripped my arm like a steel vice. I saw that he was looking over her head – upstairs. For just a second I caught a glimpse of Raymond Blair staring at him beseechingly – his hands locked together in agonised entreaty. Then the vision vanished, and once more Jim was looking gravely at the girl.

For two or three minutes she continued, speaking with biting scorn – and Jim never answered a word.

"Have you anything to say – any excuse to make?" she asked at length, and he shook his head.

"You cur!" she whispered very low. "Oh, you cur!"

Then without a backward glance she went up to her room like a young queen and we heard the door close. After a while he turned to us with a little twisted smile on his face.

"It's better so," he said gravely, "much better so."

But MacAndrew was not so easily appeased. His sense of fair play was outraged, and he said as much to Maitland.

"He lied – the cad!" he growled. "He lied to her after his promise to you. She should be told."

The smile vanished from Jim Maitland's lips, and he stared very straight at the Scotchman.

"The man who tells her," he said quietly, "answers for it to me."

And with that he swung out of the hotel.

Thus ended my first meeting with Jim Maitland. We left in the boat next day, and I saw him leaning over the stern, staring at the island till it was but a faint smudge on the horizon. Then he went to his cabin and I saw him no more till the following morning. Two days later he left the boat.

It was six months before I saw him again up in Nagasaki. He greeted me as if we had parted the day before – that was one of his peculiarities. After a while he looked at me with a faint smile.

"Been back to Tampico, Leyton?"

"No," I answered. "Have you?"

"Just come from there." He took out his pocketbook. "There's an additional ornament in the island."

He handed me a photograph, and I stared at it in silence. It was the cemetery with its rows of little wooden crosses. But in the centre rose a big white stone cross, and on it was written:

IN LOVING MEMORY
OF
RAYMOND BLAIR

"How long ago did it happen?" I asked.

"He lasted three months – and he nearly broke her heart. But she stuck it – and she never complained. MacAndrew told me. When it was over she went home to England."

"Why don't you go after her?" I said quietly, and Jim Maitland stared at the cherry tree opposite.

"'You cur!'" he said below his breath. "'Oh, you cur!' Man, I can hear her now."

He shook his head.

"She wouldn't understand, old man; she wouldn't understand. No – I'm a wanderer born and bred: and I shall wander to the end."

He glanced at his watch. "What about some dinner?"

Over the coffee the conversation took a personal turn. The death of an uncle in England had made me independent, and I was at a loose end. I had half made up my mind to go back home and buy a small property. Maitland shrugged his shoulders as I said so.

"You'll be able to do all that when you're fifty," he remarked. "Why do it now?"

"What else is there?" I asked.

He looked at me thoughtfully.

"Would you care to join forces with me?" he said at length. "As I said before, I'm a wanderer, and I go whenever and wherever the spirit moves me. But I enjoy life."

It took me one second to decide.

"I'd like it immensely," I said.

"Good," he remarked, holding out his hand. "We'll have some fun. There's a tramp going tomorrow for Colombo and the Mediterranean, and the skipper is a pal of mine. We might go in her."

"Where to?" I asked.

"Heaven knows," laughed Jim. "We'll get off when we feel inclined."

"Right you are," I said. "I'll get my kit sent down."

"How much have you got?" he demanded.

"A couple of trunks and a hand grip."

"I'd leave the two trunks and take the grip," he remarked. "A man can go round the world with a spare set of underclothes and a gun, you know."

I suppose I stared at him a little blankly, for he laughed suddenly.

"There's plenty of time for you still to take that property in England, old man."

That night the trunks were dispensed with.

CHAPTER 2

The Killing of Baron Stockmar

We left that tramp at Alexandria.

"I want to go to Shepheard's," Jim had announced, "and see all the tourists buying genuine Egyptian scarabs. I own shares in the factory that makes them."

So we went to Shepheard's, where we found a chubby-faced youth eating salted almonds and consuming something that tinkled pleasantly in a glass.

"Hullo, Pumpkin," cried Jim cheerfully from the door. "Let me introduce: Dick Leyton – Captain Peddleton, otherwise known as Pumpkin owing to his extreme slenderness."

Peddleton nodded to me.

"Jim," he said earnestly, "one of the Great Ones will be very glad to see you. Are you doing anything in the immediate future?"

"Nothing to write home about," said Jim. "I might take a tram and go out and see the Pyramids by moonlight."

"Dry up," laughed the other. Then he said seriously, "I'm not joking. It's a little Secret Service job south of Khartoum. It won't take long, but you're one of the few men in the world who can do it."

Jim grunted non-committally.

"Will you come up and see the Chief this afternoon?"

He broke off suddenly and stared at the door.

"Good heavens!" he muttered. "What have we here?"

Coming into the bar was the most unpleasant-looking individual I have ever seen in my life. His height must have been at least six-feet three, and he was broad in proportion. The man looked like a huge gorilla dressed in clothes. His face seemed set in a permanent scowl, which deepened to a look of fury as he saw us staring at him.

As luck would have it, Jim was nearest to him. He had his back turned, and was on the point of resuming his conversation, when the newcomer shoved into him heavily. In view of what we afterwards found out, I have not the slightest doubt that the thing was done deliberately. It appeared that he wanted the high stool just behind Jim, though there were several others vacant. In fact the place was empty save for the four of us.

Jim's face went white and his eyes blazed ominously. Then he turned round slowly. The newcomer was about to sit down. He did, heavily – on the floor – as the result of an old trick for which I have distinct recollections of having been severely beaten at school.

The man's face was purple as he got up. His lips were working, and his great hairy hands kept clenching and unclenching. Quite motionless, Jim stared at him through his eyeglass, to all appearances as cool as a cucumber.

"Was it you who pulled my stool away?" the man asked at length in a guttural voice which shook so that we could scarcely hear what he said.

"Was it you who deliberately barged into my back and failed to apologise?" retorted Jim icily.

Then the man broke loose. Every vestige of self-control left him.

The waiter, with a terrified look on his face, beckoned to me.

"Get your friend out of it," he whispered. "It's Baron Stockmar, and he goes stark mad if he's crossed."

There was a good deal of truth in what the waiter said. The man was not a man – he was a maniac. But as to removing Jim, I would as soon have tried to remove a leopard from its kill.

He was standing up. His breath was coming a little faster than usual, but his eyes never left the other's face. Not a word had he spoken, even when the Baron became personal. It wasn't until the Baron admitted that the collision had been no accident but an intentional insult, and launched into his private opinions of Englishmen in general, that Jim did anything. Then it was clean and decisive, and showed the perfect fighting man that he was.

The Baron's great head was thrust forward, and his two hands were coming up slowly towards Jim, when there came the sharp crisp noise as of two billiard balls meeting. With every atom of weight in his body behind the blow, Jim Maitland struck Baron Stockmar on the point of his jaw, and he crumpled up and toppled backwards.

For a moment we stood there watching the heavily breathing unconscious figure. It was then that we realised that an excited and terrified crowd of spectators had thronged in at the door.

"Get him out of here, Leyton," said Peddleton urgently in my ear. "There's going to be trouble, and we must get to the Chief at once."

We dragged him through the crowd at the door, and rushed him into the street.

"Confound you!" he grumbled. "That brute hasn't apologised yet."

"Doesn't matter, old man," laughed Peddleton. Not till we turned into the officers' mess at Kasrel-Nil, did Peddleton breathe freely again.

"Sit down, Jim," he said then. "I want to talk to you for a moment, and then I'm going to take you straight up to the Chief. I didn't realise who he was until I heard what the waiter told Leyton. He's a gentleman about whose coming we've been warned. There are diplomatic reasons, Jim, which render it a little unfortunate that you removed that seat. Diplomatically, old man, it was unfortunate."

Peddleton's good-natured face was looking quite worried. He got to his feet.

"Look here, Jim, come along and see the Chief, now. Leyton, you won't mind waiting here, will you? Shout for anything you want."

"Can you leave for Khartoum with me tonight?" Jim asked me later that day.

"I can," I answered. Then my curiosity got the better of me. "What's happened?"

"The Pumpkin was right," he said. "Unofficially the Chief kissed me on both cheeks, so to speak; officially he cursed me into fourteen different heaps. There are certain things I can't tell you, but our friend the gorilla is the accredited agent of a certain government. He has arrived, apparently, on some question of trade concessions in the Sudan, and he is not welcome even officially.

"The funny thing is that the job the Pumpkin was speaking to me about this morning is concerned directly with him. It is to frustrate the very thing he has come out to do, and it must be done unofficially. Hence, me. I have been told unofficially exactly what the Chief wants officially – and I leave tonight."

A lazy grin spread over his face. "I gather Baron Carl Stockmar proposes to visit Khartoum in the near future."

"Things become clearer," I murmured. "Jim, the man's mad."

He shrugged his shoulders.

"His principal hatred," he said, "is for the English. I trust most fervently that we shall renew our friendship in Khartoum."

The grin had faded from his face.

Now I come to the second and final act of the drama. It is the first time that the facts have been put on paper, though many shrewd guesses were made by officers of the Royal South Sussex, quartered at Khartoum.

One thing I would say at the beginning, and that is that von Tarnim of the 3rd Regiment of the Prussian Guard was a sahib. He was forced into an unenviable position simply because he was a Prussian officer, and there was no one else to take his place.

But I am jumping ahead. Four weeks after we left Cairo we returned to Khartoum. On the way through we had dined with the South Sussex, and at dinner Jim had hinted to the Colonel the nature of his business.

The next day we went into the wilds, and of the next three weeks there is nothing to tell. Jim talked to many strange dignified men in their own lingo. Every one of them seemed to know him as an old friend. They suggested sport, but Jim smiled and refused, and pushed on deeper into the desert.

Then came the day when we turned and retraced our steps. The job he had been sent to do was done; the results were locked in Jim's brain. I didn't ask questions, but I knew he was satisfied. Only once did he allude to it, and that was the night before we reached Khartoum. "I think, old son," he remarked, "that we have checkmated the dear Baron."

Next evening we arrived, and dined quietly at the hotel. After dinner we strolled over to the South Sussex mess. That the Baron was dining there as an official guest we did not know; that he had interviewed a stately Prince of the desert during the course of the day, and had met with a firm refusal to certain propositions he advanced, we had even less idea. This refusal, the first-fruits of Jim's mission, had thrown the Baron into a white heat of rage. The concessions had not gone a month ago, he roared furiously; how did it happen they had gone now? And the grave Bedouin had shrugged his shoulders and stalked from the room.

Baron Stockmar, arriving at the South Sussex mess for dinner, was still in the same mood. He was not the man to take such a thing lying down. To fail in what he had decided to do was unusual for him, and his mood at dinner was one of smouldering passion. He made no attempt at even ordinary politeness, and a general desire to sling him out of the mess became prevalent before the soup was finished. One thing the Baron did with gusto – he punished the champagne until even the Colonel began to look uneasy.

Then came the first unpleasant episode. The cloths were removed, and the officers were waiting for the toast.

"Gentlemen – the King."

Every officer rose – but not so the Baron. There were a few moments of icy silence, then the Colonel spoke quietly.

"We are about to drink the health of our King, Baron Stockmar. May I request you to stand up."

The Baron rose. There was something in the ring of furious men who were staring at him that warned even him not to go too far...

It was into this atmosphere that Jim and I blundered later on. The Baron was sitting with his back to us, and we neither of us noticed him. All we saw was a bunch of officers looking about as cheerful as a crowd of deaf-mutes.

Jim looked at them in surprise.

"Why so merry and bright?" he cried cheerfully. "Having returned from a most successful trip in the wilds, and seen all my old pals, including Mahomet Ali, we've come up to play hunt the slipper."

Mahomet Ali was the man whom the Baron had seen that afternoon. He rose from his chair and faced Jim. Whether or not he realised that it was Jim who had forestalled him I do not know, but on his face was the look of a maniac. He walked towards Jim, swaying slightly.

"You struck me a little while ago," he said thickly. "Then you ran like an Englishman. Will this force you to give me the satisfaction one gentleman demands of another?"

And he flung the contents of his glass straight in Jim's face.

The only man in the room who seemed completely unmoved was Jim, as he mopped his face, polished his eyeglass, and replaced it.

"Dear me, Colonel," he remarked at length, "I wondered what had become of that gorilla. I can't congratulate you on the manners you've taught it. I shall have to take the brute in hand myself."

With a snarl the Baron hurled himself at Jim, and for a moment my heart stood still. Immensely powerful though Jim was, at close quarters he could not have stood a chance. But once again I had reckoned without my man. As Baron Stockmar rushed at him, he dived forward and tackled him below the knees. It was a perfect Rugby tackle, and the Baron's head in falling hit the edge of the piano. They left him where he lay.

"That is the second time, sir," said Jim to the Colonel. "The world is not big enough for this gentleman."

"Careful, Jim," said the Colonel. "Don't get yourself into any trouble, old boy."

"You can't go having any fool tricks with revolvers, Jim," said the second in command. "Duelling isn't allowed in His Majesty's domain."

"Nevertheless, Tubby, old man," said Jim quietly, "I shall deal with him. Shall we leave it at that? I don't think you had better ask any questions."

At that moment the Baron staggered to his feet.

"You will hear further from me, sir," he said shakily.

"I should hate to think so," answered Jim coldly. "There's the door."

No one spoke till the sound of his swaying footsteps had died away; then the Colonel again shook his head.

"Jim," he said earnestly, "I entreat you to be careful. You will put me in an awful position if…"

"Colonel," said Jim quietly, "did you hear what he said? – 'I ran like an Englishman.'"

His voice shook a little; then he went on quietly: "If he apologises before you all for his remark, I am prepared to let the matter drop. Otherwise, as I said before, you had better ask no questions."

At that moment the mess-sergeant flung open the door of the ante-room, and ushered in a tall fair-haired man who held himself stiffly.

"Mr Maitland?" he said.

"That's me," remarked Jim.

"I am Count von Tarnim of the 3rd Regiment of the Prussian Guard. I am here on behalf of Baron Stockmar. Is there any gentleman here who is acting for you, and to whom I can speak? I presume you have guessed my mission."

"I certainly have," said the Colonel quietly. "And you must quite understand, Count, that anything in the nature of duelling is strictly forbidden under English law, and that I, as the senior military officer here, flatly forbid it."

Count von Tarnim bowed.

"I understand, sir," he answered. "I am to give that message to my principal, am I, Mr Maitland?"

"You are," said Jim. "And when you've given that message, Mr Leyton here will be delighted to discuss the prospects of sport a little farther up the White Nile."

Count von Tarnim bowed again, and the suspicion of a smile hovered round his lips.

"I shall find Mr Leyton – where?" he asked.

"At the hotel," I answered, and with another stiff bow he left the mess.

It was an hour later that Count von Tarnim came up to me in the hotel.

"My principal wishes to know when and where he may expect satisfaction," said the Count abruptly.

"Precisely," I answered. "I am not well up in the etiquette of these matters, but I may say at once what my principal has decided. As duelling is forbidden, he has chosen big-game rifles. He proposes that we should all go after lions to some suitable place. He then proposes that your principal and he should take cover as directed by us. They stalk each other until a result takes place. Should that result prove fatal, the survivor, for his own sake, is not likely to talk about it. The vultures will do the rest. Do I make myself clear?"

"Perfectly," said von Tarnim, clicking his heels together. "I will acquaint my principal with what you have said."

With that he left me, to return in ten minutes with the information that the Baron agreed. For a moment or two he stared at me irresolutely.

"It is most unorthodox, what I am going to say," he said, with a great deal of hesitation. "I am Baron Stockmar's second, and therefore his interests are mine. But he is a peculiar man; his reputation is notorious; and I think it only fair to tell you that he is probably the finest shot in Germany. Moreover, he is quite determined to kill your friend."

He was very stiff about it. I could see the man's decent nature struggling with horror at his own breach of etiquette. The next moment his horror deepened. Jim, who had come into the room unnoticed, smote him on the back.

"Tell the Baron, with my love," he said earnestly, "that I once slaughtered a sparrow with a catapult."

Though Jim was his usual self during the two days' trek south, there was an undercurrent of seriousness beneath his gaiety. He slept, as usual, like a child, but he gave me in full the report which I was to render to the Chief in Cairo in case anything happened; also he gave me one or two private commissions.

The night before the duel he was a little more silent than usual. I had fixed the final details with von Tarnim; the spot had been duly selected. As I came back, Jim looked up with a lazy smile from oiling his rifle.

"What extraordinary fellows we are!" he remarked thoughtfully. "I don't know that it affords me any pleasure to go out and try to kill this bird tomorrow. I felt like murdering him in the mess that night, but now…"

He returned to his task and shortly afterwards we turned in. I know who slept the worse.

Even the next morning Jim seemed bored. He told me afterwards that he'd lost interest in the affair, and all the smouldering fury in Baron Stockmar's eyes failed to rouse him. When I showed him the place we had selected, he lounged about as if he were looking for butterflies.

"He means business, Jim," I said urgently. "He's blind mad with rage still."

"Is he?" said Jim indifferently. "That will make him shoot the worse."

They were to start when we fired a revolver, and von Tarnim gave the signal as soon as they were ready. We were standing on a little sandy hummock above the scrub, whence we could see both men though they could not see one another. Then began the grimmest fight that it has ever been my fortune to witness. Von Tarnim beside me was smoking cigarette after cigarette; I was chewing an empty pipe.

Occasionally a shot rang out, but it seemed to me that Jim was taking things too easily. Once I saw a bullet flatten itself on a stone not an inch from Jim's head.

He was just underneath us at the moment and he drew back quickly. Then he looked at the stone very carefully and I saw his face change. Through my glasses I could see the look of boredom vanish, and I breathed a sigh of relief. Something had roused him at last, turned him from a bored man into a grim and ruthless hunter. At a quick lope he turned and vanished into the scrub. Every now and then we saw him listening intently; every now and then we saw the great figure of the Baron squirming forward, his head turning from side to side as he peered into the undergrowth.

Suddenly von Tarnim gripped my arm convulsively; the two men were not more than twenty yards apart. A big bush was between them, but we could see them both. At that moment each became aware of the other. Like a flash Jim was round the bush. He fired standing, the fraction of a second before the other. Then he spun round and sank on his knees, while von Tarnim and I raced towards them.

I raised Jim in my arms; the Baron had shot him through the shoulder. It was a dreadful wound, and I stared at it in amazement.

Suddenly Jim opened his eyes and stared at me.

"He was using dum-dums," he said. "Dum-dums!"

We looked up at Count von Tarnim. He had heard Jim's remark, and his face was stern.

"I apologise in the name of my country," he said with quiet dignity. "My principal cannot."

For the first time I looked at the Baron – and understood.

CHAPTER 3

A Game of Bluff

It was three months before Jim came out of hospital, and even then his arm was stiff. The expanding bullet had torn the ligaments badly, and for quite a time the doctor had looked grave.

"A long course of electric massage is essential," he said emphatically. "Otherwise I warn you seriously that your arm may remain like that permanently. There's a wonderful new man in Paris: I'll give you his name if you like."

"We might do worse, Dick," remarked Jim. "They tell me that there are worse places."

"Confound you!" I said. "What about those two trunks of perfectly good clothes I left in Nagasaki?"

"What about your perfectly good uncle," he laughed, "who has left you all his money? Besides, we shall probably never get as far as Paris – so nothing matters."

We started anyway, and, amazing to relate, in the fullness of time we got there. But we had a little upset on the way which might have ended very unpleasantly but for Jim. It bore out in a rather remarkable manner one of his theories on life.

Jim is the least dogmatic man in the world, but there are certain things on which he holds very definite opinions – very definite. Some of those opinions are hardly everybody's money, but they are all worth listening to. The particular one to which I am alluding is his theory on the matter of Bluff; and since you can't get through life without bluff, it may be worth while stating it, as I once heard Jim state it to a youngster who asked his advice.

"Bluff, my son, is winning an unlimited jackpot with a queen high hand from a fellow with three aces, and upsetting the table before you can be asked to show your openers. Bluff, my lad, is getting a man with a gun pointed at the pit of your stomach to look the other way for just long enough to allow you to alter the target. Bluff, my boy, is, in short, the art of winning a game with losing cards, and the essence of that art is to play the hand right through as if you held winners, without a thought of failure. Not a touch of hesitation, not a moment of doubt."

If ever there was a case when a game was won with losing cards, the affair at Monte Carlo was it.

When we left Port Said in a home-going P & O we never intended going near the place. Paris was our destination via Marseilles; but you never can tell.

Incidentally the purser's humour had something to do with it, if such great beings as pursers have anything to do with arranging menus. The Gulf of Lyons was at its worst, which means that food needed choosing with care. To select pork chops for dinner simply showed a fiendish ingenuity not far short of diabolical. In tens and dozens weeping women and frenzied men lurched from the dining saloon, until but a bare score of hardened sinners were left trying to conceal their unseemly mirth.

It was the uncontrolled joy of a very pretty girl sitting two tables away from us that principally attracted our attention. I had noticed an elderly man who had been sitting beside her rise suddenly and depart with a fixed and glassy stare in his eyes. It was an ill wind in more senses than one, for his place was immediately taken by a boy who moved up from the other end of the table.

We knew the boy slightly – a great youngster by the name of Jack Rawson. He was in cotton at Alexandria, a junior member of one of the big firms, and he was returning to England on business. After a while Jim turned to me with a faint smile and then looked across again at the pair of them.

"The only story in the world," he remarked, "that is older than sea-sickness."

"Who is the girl?" I asked.

"An Australian, I think. Jack told me her name. Mother is at Nice, and I suppose the bird who fled from the crackling is Father."

We finished our dinner and went above. She was pitching very badly in a long following swell, and for an hour or so we strolled up and down the almost deserted deck. It wasn't until we were thinking of turning in that we stumbled on Jack Rawson and the girl snugly ensconced in a sheltered corner. We tried to get away unnoticed, but the boy hailed Jim at once.

"Maitland," he cried, "I want to introduce you to Miss Melville, my fiancée."

Jim bowed gravely and smiled.

"My heartiest congratulations," he remarked. "A pork chop is sometimes a godsend, isn't it?"

"Poor old Daddy!" said the girl with quick remorse. "I had forgotten all about him. But I couldn't help laughing, because he always tells everyone he's never been sick in his life. I'd better go and see how he is."

"From my knowledge of the complaint," said Jim, "I don't think he'll thank you. Complete seclusion is generally the victim's one demand of life."

So she stopped, and for a few minutes we talked. Young Jack, we gathered, was getting off at Marseilles and going to meet her mother at Nice. Then he was going back overland to arrive in London at the same time as he would have done if he had stuck to the boat. Then the question of his father would crop up. In fact, fathers loomed rather large on the horizon. For the engagement had only been fixed that night, and Mr Melville was also in ignorance of the devastating effects of pork chops on the young and healthy.

That was where the trouble came in. Would he have sufficiently recovered by the following morning to make it advisable to spring the news on him? Or would he regard it as a mean advantage, taken while he was otherwise employed? It was undoubtedly a point demanding careful consideration. So much depends on the way these matters are approached.

The girl was doubtful. She was convinced that next morning would be fully occupied in listening to his explanations that it was not the rough sea which had caused his indisposition, but that his fish at lunch had been slightly stale. The moment would not be opportune, she was sure. That being the case, why should Jack suddenly alter his plan of going home by sea, and come to Nice? In fact, what was to he done? How could Jack come to Nice in an easy natural manner which should cause no suspicion on the part of her paternal parent, and at the same time allow the news of the engagement to be broken at a more favourable time?

We discussed the knotty point at some length, until Jim suddenly settled things in his usual direct way. He and I would also break our journey at Marseilles and go to Nice, or rather to Monte Carlo, and Jack would come with us. It was, as he remarked, part of every man's education to see the Casino, and more especially the people who frequented it; and since Jack had never seen it, it was high time he did so. If Jack was foolish enough to prefer going over to Nice and sitting in the sunshine with his girl rather than haunting a roulette table – well, the point hardly arose at that stage of the proceedings.

With that we left them, cutting short their thanks, and retired to the smoking-room. Half an hour later, as we turned in, I saw them still sitting in their secluded corner, dreaming great dreams in a world of their own.

We did not see much of young Jack during the next three or four days. We lounged about the terrace, and had a mild flutter or two at the tables. But the place irked terribly. It was so intensely artificial. Jim particularly sickened of it.

"By Jove, Dick," he said to me on the fourth night of our stay, "I've seen more wickedness in my life than most of the people here put together, but I don't believe there's a place in the whole world where quite so much rottenness is concealed beneath a beautiful surface as in Monte.

"I suppose they think it's worth it," he remarked. "But what a price to pay! I'm no moralist, but I like things big. Big virtues; big sins if you like. But in this place the only big thing is the price."

Then he fell silent and stared over my shoulder.

"Hallo!" he went on slowly, "here's Jack Rawson. And something has happened."

I turned round and saw the boy coming towards us. He was walking unevenly, and on his face was a look of hopeless despair.

"Well, young fellow," said Jim quietly as he came abreast of us, "what's the worry?"

Jack paused, and seemed to see us for the first time. Then, with a quick shake of his head, he made as if to pass on. But he had gone only a step or two when Jim's hand fell on his shoulder and spun him round.

"Let me go, confound you!" muttered the boy.

"All in good time, old man," said Jim in the same quiet voice. "Just at the moment I think a little talk will clear the air."

He forced Jack to a seat between us, and suddenly put his hand into the boy's coat pocket.

"This won't help, Jack," he said a little sternly, and I saw that he had a small revolver in his hand. "That's never the way out, except for a coward."

It was then that the boy broke down, and I caught Jim's eye over the shaking shoulders. It was savage and angry, as if he realised, even then, that we were in the presence of another of those rotten little tragedies which have their breeding ground in those few square miles. Jack pulled himself together after a few seconds, and lit a cigarette while we waited in silence. Bit by bit the whole sordid story came out – as old as the hills and yet new in every fresh case.

The engagement was all right, we found out, as far as her father and mother were concerned. The only question had been one of money. Her father didn't think that Jack's income was sufficient to allow of marrying yet; further, he thought that in view of the shortness of their acquaintance a little waiting would be a good thing from every point of view. He wouldn't go so far as to say that if Jack had actually had the money he would have insisted on a long engagement, but since he hadn't, he thought it was much the most satisfactory solution.

Just after this interview with Mr Melville Jack met a very charming Frenchman in Nice. He was the Count de St Enogat, and they had entered into conversation.

It was at this stage of the disclosure that Jim's eye again met mine.

Apparently one cocktail had been followed by another; and then a third and fourth. Jack, drawn on by his new friend's delightful and sympathetic manner, had taken the charming Count into his confidence. After four cocktails – or was it five? – the problem was a simple one. The girl's father – a silly old fool – insisted that he should have more money before he could marry his daughter. How was he to get that money quickly and certainly? Any idea of waiting was simply unthinkable. After five – or was it six? – the solution to the problem was even simpler.

The Count, touched to the very core of his French soul by such a wonderful tale of devotion and love, would do for this new friend what he had never before done for any human being. Locked in the Count's heart was a system – *the* system – *the only* system by which one could with absolute certainty make money by gambling. If Jack would come with him that afternoon, he would take him to a private gambling place where he guaranteed, on his word as a member of the French nobility, that Jack would win enough money to snap his fingers at the idiotic father of his lovely fiancée.

Jim's eyes met mine for the third time.

He lunched at the expense of his new friend – lightly, with a bottle of champagne; and then proceeded in the Count's powerful Delage to a villa half-way between Nice and Monte Carlo – a charming villa, we gathered, where he was introduced to one or two of the Count's friends. After a short while the Count suggested an adjournment for business. There was roulette in one room, and baccarat in another. Petits-chevaux, poker and even fan-tan seemed to be legislated for, each in its own separate room. But the great point over which Jack was most insistent was the singular charm of everyone he met.

"Quite so," cut in Jim shortly, as he paused. "I'm sure they were. But to come down to more prosaic details – which game did you patronise?"

"Baccarat," said the boy. "The Count advised it."

"Holy smoke!" muttered Jim. "Baccarat! Yes, I can quite imagine he did advise it!"

"He said it was the easiest to make money at by his system."

"Undoubtedly," answered Jim. "Quite the easiest to make money at – for him. Now, Jack, what did you lose?"

The boy hesitated.

"Out with it," said Jim. "You've been a triple-distilled young fool, but there's no good mincing things now."

"A hundred thousand francs," answered Jack, almost inaudibly; and, leaning forward, he buried his face in his hands.

Jim raised his eyebrows. A hundred thousand francs was four thousand pounds in those days before currencies went mad, and the same thought came to both of us: where had young Jack Rawson found four thousand pounds to lose?

"Did you give them a cheque?" asked Jim quietly.

Then, slowly and hesitatingly, the real trouble came out. He hadn't given them a cheque – it wouldn't have been honoured if he had. But he had been entrusted with twenty thousand pounds' worth of bearer bonds in some Egyptian Government security to take home and hand over to the head office of the firm in London. Why the matter had been done that way we did not inquire; the mere bald fact stuck out and was sufficient.

Jack Rawson had lost four thousand pounds of money which belonged to his firm, playing baccarat; and since the actual loss was in bearer bonds, not even the replacing of the money could save him from detection. Nothing short of regaining the actual scrip could be of any use. Unless that was done, it meant disgrace and ruin for the boy sitting miserably between us.

So much was clear on the face of it, and for a while we sat in silence staring over the bay.

"I was a bit drunk," he stammered miserably at length, "otherwise I wouldn't have been such a darned fool. But he seemed such a good sort, and all I could think of was getting enough to marry Peggy."

With that he broke down utterly; it meant losing his girl as well.

"When did it happen, Jack?" said Jim quietly.

"This afternoon," answered the boy.

"You'd know the house again?" pursued Jim.

"Only too well," muttered Jack, miserably throwing pebbles into a flower-bed opposite.

Suddenly he straightened up and gripped Jim by the arm.

"Look, Maitland," he cried excitedly, "there's the man himself. There's the Count."

He half rose, but Jim pulled him back.

"Sit down," he said quietly. "Bend forward. Don't let him see you with us. Do you mean that man in evening clothes, walking with the girl in the scarlet cloak?"

"Yes," answered the boy.

We watched him as he ascended some steps a few yards to our left and turned with his companion towards the Casino. He looked, as Jack had said, a charming man, a typical French aristocrat in Monte Carlo during the height of the season.

Jim thoughtfully lit a cigarette and sat for a while in silence. Then, as if he had made up his mind, he rose to his feet and pitched his cigarette away.

"Go back to the hotel," he said curtly, "and turn in. I'll see what I can do."

It was typical of Jim that he added no word of reproach, and at once cut short the stammered thanks of the boy, in whose eyes hope was already beginning to dawn.

"Cut all that out," he remarked. "I don't promise that I'll be able to do anything, but I'll see. And remember one thing: if you meet either Leyton or myself tomorrow or at any time with the Count, you don't know either of us. Don't forget. Now clear off."

For a moment he laid his hands on the boy's shoulders, then he turned him round and pushed him towards the hotel.

"Silly young ass!" he said to me as Rawson disappeared round a corner. "But he's a good boy for all that. And she's a good girl."

"It's a bit of a tough proposition, Jim," I remarked dubiously.

"I don't deny it," he answered. "At the moment I haven't an idea how to set about it. This place may be a sink of iniquity, but anything in the nature of gunwork would render one unpopular. No, it's got to be something more subtle than that. The first thing to do, however, is to cultivate the acquaintance of the Count. The second is to go to this house. I think we had better separate for the time, old man, though we might join up later in the evening. I'll go on into the Casino now. You come in in a few minutes.

34

Then be guided by circumstances. We just know each other, that's all."

With a cheery grin he strolled away, with that merry gleam in his eyes which was never absent if an adventure was on the cards. I watched him enter the Casino, and five minutes after I followed him.

I strolled round the rooms casually, but he seemed to have disappeared, and after a while I tried the bar. Sure enough, there was Jim with a dangerous-looking drink in front of him, the Count on one side and the charming girl in the scarlet cloak on the other. The trio were in a convivial mood.

At least Jim was. Had I been asked to go into a court of law and give evidence as to Jim's condition, I should have said that he was in that happy mood which comes from having drunk enough but not too much. It was evident that the game had begun.

As soon as he saw me he hailed me cheerfully.

"Hullo, Leyton, old lad," he cried. "Come and join us. A pal of mine, Mademoiselle – also from the ends of the earth."

I bowed to the girl and sat down opposite Jim.

"I've just been telling the Count – oh, by the way, the Count de St Enogat – Mr Leyton – that I can't stand these rooms here. Too crowded altogether. I like gambling high; I can afford to gamble high. I've gambled in every corner of this little old globe, and there's not much I don't know about it. But I can't stand a crush. Hi, you, whatever your name is – repeat the dose, my lad."

"And I have just been telling your friend, Mr Leyton," said the Count, with a charming smile, "that if he wants a quiet game, with stakes high or low as he pleases – "

"High for me," interrupted Jim. "I'm not playing halfpenny nap."

The Count bowed, and his smile broadened.

"No, Mr Maitland, as a fair judge of men, I guessed that. Well, you can take it from me that you can play as high as you like, in perfect peace and quiet, and not with this crowd round you, if you care to come with Mademoiselle St Quentin and myself to a villa a few kilometres on the road to Nice. Every form of game you can want is there, run for people exactly like yourself – people who prefer peace and quiet. You can play bridge if you like, or poker, or baccarat, or roulette."

Jim leant across the table to me.

"Leyton," he said, "did you hear that? These guys play poker. What about it?"

He winked deliberately and the Count smiled again.

"There are two men there who play poker most nights and rather fancy themselves."

"They do?" grunted Jim. "I'll come and play poker with them."

For a fleeting instant the Count's eyes met the girl's; then he rose.

"My car is at the door. Will Mr Leyton come?"

"I'm with you," I said, finishing my drink. "But I warn you that I'm not a gambler like my friend."

"All tastes are catered for, Mr Leyton," said the girl, speaking for the first time. But I noticed she was watching Jim as he strolled with the Count through the rooms towards the entrance. "Is he very wealthy, your friend?"

"Rolls in it," I murmured.

"He looks a very determined sort of person," she remarked.

"He's as peaceful as a lamb," I answered. "A married man with four children."

"I hope he wins," she said. "It's high time those two men lost, for a change."

With that we got into the car.

I had no inkling of what Jim proposed to do; and as he left me almost at once on arriving at the house, and repaired to the poker room with the Count, I had no opportunity of a private word with him. So I contented myself with a little mild roulette and kept my eyes open.

The whole thing was beautifully done, of that there was no doubt. The champagne was first-class and unlimited; the whole house gave one the idea that everything had been done regardless of expense. There were some twenty people in the roulette room, and, though play was high, I could see no suspicion of anything unfair. Nor for that matter at the baccarat table in another room, where I staked a few louis and won. In fact, it struck me that the whole place was what it professed to be – a first-class gambling-house where stakes were high.

My lady in the scarlet cloak, in the intervals of being very charming, pumped me discreetly about Jim, and I played up along the lines that he had started. It was quite obvious that I was regarded as the necessary encumbrance to the real quarry, and the idea was just what I wanted. Jim was rich, Jim was the gambler, Jim was the fish to be landed. Once or twice I almost laughed as I thought of the particular wolf who had strayed into the fold.

The sheep's clothing was still there two hours later when Jim appeared with the Count. A cheerful but somewhat inane grin was on his face, and he stumbled once – very slightly. It was a magnificent imitation of a man who had drunk just a little too much, and once again I saw the Count's eyes meet my companion's with a hint of triumph in them.

"Cleaned me out, Leyton," cried Jim, slapping the Count on the back. "Ten thousand francs, my boy – but that's only a bagatelle. Tomorrow afternoon we'll begin to play. Now, Count – you'll lunch with me, and you too, Mademoiselle. I simply insist. Just the four of us, and afterwards we'll come back here. I'll show you tomorrow how poker should be played."

"You had infernal luck, Mr Maitland," said the Count politely. "Tomorrow you will have your revenge. And lunch – at one?"

"One o'clock. I shall expect you both." He bowed over the girl's hand. "You shall sit beside me tomorrow afternoon, Mademoiselle, and bring me luck."

The Count insisted on sending us home in his Delage, and all the way back Jim talked loudly for the benefit of the chauffeur.

It was not until we were in our rooms that the mask dropped and he was himself again.

"It's crooked, Dick," he said quietly. "They swindled me tonight. I saw 'em of course – the old trick of substituting a similar pack after the cut. They dealt me a flush, and the Count drew one to threes, and got four eights. I betted as if I hadn't noticed."

"The roulette and baccarat were perfectly straight as far as I could see," I said.

"Probably," he answered. "It's more than likely that for ninety per cent of the time the thing is straight. It's only when they get hold of a plum that they risk the other. And mark you, it was well done. If I hadn't forgotten more than these fellows are ever likely to know, I wouldn't have noticed it."

He was pacing up and down the room thoughtfully, pulling hard at his pipe.

"I can't think what to do, Dick," he cried at length. "Gunwork is out of the question, and the mere statement that someone is cheating, even if you prove it then and there on the spot, is no use when you're up against a gang. Righteous indignation: the cheater would be indignantly kicked out, and one's losses would be refunded. Mark you, it wasn't the Count who cheated; he wasn't dealing. But the new pack was stacked so that he got the hand. They were all in it – all four of them. I can smell a thing like that better than a cat smells fish. And it's going to be the same bunch tomorrow. The point is what to do."

He resumed his thoughtful pacing.

"Bluff! Some sort of bluff! But what? How can I bluff that bunch – how can I bluff the Count into disgorging those bonds?"

Suddenly he stopped, his eyes blazing.

"I've got it," he almost shouted. "Go to bed, Dick. I've got to work out the details."

With that he bundled me out, and when I turned out my light I could still hear him pacing up and down. But when I went into his room next morning about half-past ten he had already gone out, and I didn't see him again until twenty minutes before lunch.

He grinned at me and we sat down in a corner.

"Got it worked out?" I asked.

"I think so, old man," he answered with a faint chuckle. "And it's best for you to know nothing about it until the time comes. But there's one thing you can do for me. Let Mademoiselle know that though I am a lamb as a rule, things happen if I get roused. Hint at dark doings in strange corners of the globe: corpses littering up rooms – you know."

"Is this part of the plan?" I asked.

"A very necessary part," he answered quietly. "And here, if I mistake not, are our guests."

We met them in the lounge and adjourned at once to lunch. It was a merry meal, during which Jim accounted for more than his fair share of the wine. I noticed that the Count drank sparingly, and his companion hardly at all. They didn't talk very much either; Jim did that.

Since Jim talks less about himself than anyone I know, it soon became evident to me that there was something in his mind. He was almost vulgar with his "I've been there, of course," and "I've seen that and done this." But because he really had been and seen and done he was also extraordinarily interesting, especially on the subject of snakes and rare native poisons. He might almost have made a study of them, so extensive was his knowledge, and Mademoiselle St Quentin shivered audibly.

"You make me quite frightened, Monsieur," she said, taking a sip of champagne. "Just one teeny scratch, you say, and a horrible death. Ugh!"

Jim laughed, and ordered another bottle.

"Such things don't come your way in civilised parts, Mademoiselle," he cried. "It's only we who have lived at the back of beyond who run across them."

"You must have had an interesting life, Mr Maitland," said the Count. "A life which many men would not have come through alive."

Jim laughed again.

"Because they don't know the secret of life, Count."

"And that is?"

"Bluff." Jim drained his glass. "Bluff. Any man can win when he's holding winners, but success only comes to the man who wins with losers. And in life – as in poker – it's bluff that enables you to do that."

The Count smiled.

"Yvonne," he said, "we have a formidable opponent this afternoon. I think I had better go to the bank and get some more money."

In due course we came once more to the house looking over the sea.

Without delay they went indoors, while I followed slowly. As a piece of acting it was superb; almost he deceived me during the next hour. Not by the quiver of an eyelid did he lapse from the character he had set himself to play – the bluff Colonial with money to lose if necessary, but with money only secondary to the game. I played more as a matter of form than anything else; my whole attention was occupied in what I knew must be coming. Gradually excitement took hold of me, till my hand grew a little unsteady and my mouth a trifle dry. If only I had known what to look out for – what to expect!

Quite suddenly it came. I had noticed nothing, but in an instant the atmosphere of the room changed to deadly fury; and, dominating them all, more furious than any, was Jim.

With a single heave he jerked the dealer from his chair, and there on the seat was the pack of cards for which the stacked pack had just been substituted.

"The same trick as last night, you bunch of sharpers!" he snarled. "Do you think I didn't spot you?"

He swung round on the Count, who, with a livid face, was backing towards the bell.

"Stand still, you!" he roared. "I'll show you how I deal with sharpers. You wretched fool – I came prepared for this."

There was a sudden sharp whistling hiss, and a long thorn-like piece of wood hung quivering from the Count's cheek.

"Put away that gun," he sneered contemptuously, as the Count produced a revolver. "Don't you understand, you wretched cheat? – you're a dead man, now. Is it beginning to prick and smart, that cheek of yours? I told you I came from the East, didn't I? And do you know what this is?"

He held out a long wooden tube, and the Count stared at it fearfully.

"That is the *sumpitan*, or blow-pipe, used by the Senangs in Malay. And that" – he pointed at the Count's cheek – "is a poisoned dart. You scum – to dare to swindle me, as you swindled that unfortunate boy out of those Egyptian bonds."

He plunged his hand into his pocket and produced a small bottle.

"There is the antidote, my friend. Don't move, or I smash it in the grate. It will add to my pleasure to see you die, watching the bottle that could save you all the time."

And now pandemonium broke loose. Two men dashed to the door, to find themselves looking down the barrel of Jim's revolver.

"I think not," he said pleasantly. "It will only be a quarter of an hour before our friend leaves us – for good. During that brief space we will all stop here."

The girl flung herself at me.

"Do something!" she screamed. "He is a savage – a monster! Beg him to save Pierre; he is my husband."

But Jim only laughed.

"Monsieur," she cried, going down on her knees to him, "I entreat of you to spare him."

Jim grunted, and lowered his revolver as if in thought.

"He is your husband, is he? Well, get me those Egyptian bonds at once. Is it smarting, Count? Then you have no time to lose, Madame. Hand me those bonds, and I will consider whether I will save this man."

He stood aside and she rushed from the room. The Count was moaning in a corner with the two other men bending over him, and Jim caught my eye and winked. So superb had been his acting, that it was only then that I began to wonder about the *sumpitan* and the poisoned dart. It occurred to me that it had looked much more like an ordinary long wooden cigarette holder.

At that moment the girl returned. Feverishly she thrust the bonds into his hands. With maddening deliberation Jim looked through them while she waited in an agony of impatience. At last he thrust them into his pocket and produced the little bottle.

"Let this be a lesson to you," he snapped. "There is the antidote. See that he drinks it all – at once."

We waited just long enough to see the contents of that bottle go down the Count's throat; then, on a quick sign from Jim, we left.

Finding the Delage waiting outside the door, it seemed but fitting that we should use it to take us back to Monte Carlo. We did.

It was not till much later on that he consented to allay my curiosity. At intervals through the afternoon he had shaken with silent laughter until he had almost driven me insane.

I knew there had been an interview with Jack, and the girl had been there too; a girl who had left with eyes misty with joy and happiness, and a boy who had left almost dazed by his good fortune.

The girl came up to me as I sat reading the paper, and I rose with a smile.

"He's just the most wonderful man in the world, Mr Leyton," she said, and her voice trembled a little.

"He is that," agreed Jack fervently.

Then I sat waiting for Jim.

He came at last, a quiet smile on his face.

"A good bluff that, Dick," he said thoughtfully.

I agreed. "What had you got on the darts?"

"Some stuff the chemist made up. Quite harmless, but it irritates abominably."

Then he started to choke with laughter.

"What's the joke?" I demanded.

"My dear old man," he spluttered, "you haven't got the plum – the supreme gem of the affair. That lies in the antidote."

I looked at him. "What the deuce was the antidote?"

"The antidote, Dick," he murmured gravely, "was just half a pint of castor-oil."

CHAPTER 4

Colette

From Paris to Valparaiso is a long call, and what started us off in that direction I can't remember. I know Jim's shoulder was a much longer job than we anticipated, but that is neither here nor there.

At Valparaiso we arrived one fine morning, and at Valparaiso we decided to stay. And in Valparaiso we ran into one of those adventures for which Jim seemed to have a special attraction.

This one nearly cost us our lives. But since it didn't quite, and moreover was responsible for a magnificent work of art, all was well. It lies before me as I write – that work of art. It consists of a photo of a family group, taken by a local photographer down in Sussex and printed on a picture postcard. Sitting on a chair is a pretty girl with happiness written all over her face, and on her lap are two remarkably healthy-looking infants. Standing behind her is the proud father arrayed in his best clothes, with a collar half an inch too small and an inch and a half too high. The girl's arms are round her babies, and it is only when I look very closely that I can notice the difference between those two arms. For the right one was splintered, and the splintering saved us from death, and the girl from a fate far worse, though even now she probably hardly realises it; which is just as well.

The thing happened in MacTavert's, which flaring lights in the street outside proclaim to be a dancing saloon. Actually, as Bully

MacTavert knew – none better – the principal source of income came from sailors just in from a voyage. When a man has taken forty days merely to get a wind-jammer round the Horn, on the top of the rest of the voyage, and has then beaten up the west coast of South America towards Valparaiso, he is apt to run a bit wild. There's money to burn in their pockets, and when it's finished a crew will be wanted for some other boat. So until then –

The dancing girls at MacTavert's were on a par with the place – and they were MacTavert's slaves. He fed them, housed them, bought them their tawdry finery; he did everything but give them money. Money makes for independence – and that was the last thing MacTavert wanted.

Not often does one find a man so completely dead to every sense of human decency as he was. Originally, as his name implied, he was a Scotsman. Just about forty-eight years ago he had first seen the light of day in a Glasgow slum. There may be kind-hearted people who will say that he never had a chance; maybe he didn't. Born and nurtured in the gutter, at ten years old he was a hardened young ruffian. At fifteen he went to sea in the three-masted ship *Celandine*, and Glasgow saw him no more. At thirty he started on his own in Valparaiso.

He began small; but now, eighteen years later, the small stuffy saloon in which he had started had grown into a big garish dancing hall, while its owner, heavy-jowled and gross, looked on his creation with beady eyes and found it good. His customers remained substantially the same, but many more could be accommodated. Therefore, to draw in the extra public he needed, the good MacTavert employed touts to haunt the town on the look-out for gullible people who wanted to "see the sights" – people who paid anything up to ten times the regular tariff without a murmur. And MacTavert himself would welcome the poor fools with an expansive smile which displayed his yellow teeth to the full advantage.

It was one of these touts who approached Jim and me before dinner. We neither of us knew Valparaiso, but that tout had "tout" written altogether too largely all over him, and Jim dealt with him with commendable brevity.

And then there occurred one of those things which a man ignores or does not ignore, according to the particular brand he is. When a woman gives a little cry for help, it may be advisable to leave matters to the proper authorities to deal with.

But that was not Jim. He swung round, and the next instant I was standing alone. When I came up with him again, the tout was struggling in his grasp, and Jim was staring over his head at a girl on the pavement beyond. She was a pretty thing, but what struck me most was the look of terror in her eyes as she glanced at the man Jim was holding.

"Can I help you in any way?" said Jim, in Spanish. "I thought I heard you call out."

She looked at Jim and her mouth drooped.

"It doesn't matter," she said, despairingly. "I thought you were English."

Jim smiled.

"I most certainly am," he answered. "I must blame the bad light for not seeing that you are, too."

Then he looked at the man who was still struggling in his grasp.

"That being the case," he continued, "how comes it that a Dago made you cry out for help? Dagos who annoy English girls are simply asking for trouble, aren't they, you repulsive little beast?"

The Dago squirmed in his hands, and Jim smiled placidly. Then he took him by the collar and the seat of his trousers and fairly slung him across the road. He lay for a moment where he fell; then with a venomous look on his face vanished down the road, and Jim turned back to the girl.

"Now, what can I do for you?"

She was gazing at him in admiration, and then she clapped her hands together.

"Oh, but you're strong!" she said. "That little brute ought to be killed. He's one of MacTavert's men."

"So I gathered," said Jim quietly. "A little while ago he was suggesting that we should go there this evening."

The girl shuddered, and once again the look of terror came into her eyes as she began to speak breathlessly.

"It's an awful place – a ghastly place. Somehow I knew you were English, and I thought perhaps you might be able to help me. That's why that little brute tried to interfere and prevent me speaking to you."

"But why should he object?" said Jim, looking a trifle puzzled. "What has he got to do with you, anyway?"

"I'm in the most dreadful trouble," said the girl, and her lips were trembling. "You see, I'm at MacTavert's."

"You're at MacTavert's?" repeated Jim slowly. "But why are you at such a place?"

"I was told to go there last night. I had no money, and I met a woman who said she could give me a room, and it didn't matter about paying her. Then I found that it was at this awful dancing saloon."

Jim looked at her gravely.

"Then why not go away?" he said at length. "Surely there must be a British chaplain here, or somebody to whom you could apply."

"But I can't find my box, or any of my things." The girl was on the verge of tears. "They've taken them away and hidden them. I don't know anyone in this horrible town, and I can't speak Spanish."

"I see," said Jim quietly. "Well, what do you want me to do?"

"If only I could tell you my story!" she cried. "But it's getting late, and I haven't got time now. I must get back, or that brute will find out I've gone, and get in a rage. You see, he told me I wasn't to go out unless he said I might. Oh, if you could come to the place tonight, and tell MacTavert you want to dance with me – That's what I have to do, you see: dance with anyone who wants me to. Then I could tell you, and perhaps you could help me."

"All right," Jim said quietly. "We'll come, and you shall tell us all about it. Then we'll see what we can do."

"Oh, thank you a thousand times!" cried the girl, dabbing at her eyes with a handkerchief. "You know where it is, don't you? Just down the road there."

"We'll find it," said Jim. "Now you trot along. By the way, what is your name?"

"Colette," said the girl simply, and she gave Jim a look such as a dog gives its master. Then she was gone, flitting like a shadow through the trees that lined the road.

For a few moments Jim watched her: then he turned to me.

"I may be several sorts of a fool, Dick," he remarked, "but I'll take my oath that wasn't a put-up job. In fact, I'm thinking we may be just in time to prevent a tragedy."

"You'll probably find MacTavert a fairly tough customer," I said, as we strolled back.

Jim grinned. "I like 'em tough. Let's dine."

He was silent during dinner, and it was not until we had nearly finished that he spoke.

"If it's what I think it is, Dick, Mr MacTavert and I will have words tonight."

His voice was savage.

MacTavert's dancing saloon took very little finding. As we entered the doors, the strains of an automatic piano grinding out a waltz met our ears, and for a moment or two we stood just inside watching the scene. It was typical of scores of similar places to be met with in seaports all over the world – a little larger than the average, but with nothing to distinguish it from a hundred others. A general reek of perspiring humanity and stale spirits filled the air. The thick haze of tobacco smoke made it almost impossible to see across the room. In the centre, where a space had been left, five or six couples were dancing. Around the walls, seated at little tables, were men of every nationality, drinking. Every now and then a couple would solemnly gyrate to the strains of the piano. Then the pair would sit down again, and more drink would be ordered.

"Good heavens, Jim!" I muttered in disgust. "What a horrible spot!"

As I spoke we saw Colette. She was dancing with a big Dago, and her eyes lit up as she saw us.

Jim smiled at her, and at that moment MacTavert himself approached. His shrewd eyes had soon discerned two toffs standing by the door, and he had no intention of letting them escape if he could help it. He bowed, showing his tobacco-stained teeth in a smile. Jim regarded him in silence.

"And what can I do for you gentlemen?" said MacTavert. "There is a good table unoccupied at the other end of the room, and I think I may say that my whisky is good. Or champagne, if you prefer it," he added hopefully.

"Show us the table," said Jim curtly, and we followed MacTavert across the room.

"Now bring me some whisky," he continued when we were seated.

"Certainly, sir," returned the other. "And if there is any lady you want to dance with, you have merely to mention the matter to me."

"There is," said Jim quietly. "That girl over there dancing with that Dago. Tell her that my friend and I will be honoured if she will join us at our table."

MacTavert rubbed his hands together; things were progressing altogether to his fancy.

"Leave it all to me," he remarked confidentially. "And if" – his voice sank to a whisper – "you would care to smoke a pipe – " He paused meaningly.

"I don't go in for opium," said Jim shortly. "Get my whisky."

For a moment MacTavert's eyes gleamed angrily; he was not used to being spoken to in such a way. But a second glance at Jim's face decided him that speech would be unwise, and with a further bow he left us.

We saw him approach the table where Colette was sitting, and speak to her. She rose instantly and followed MacTavert across the room, leaving her late dancing partner scowling furiously. But he said nothing: it was pretty evident that what MacTavert said was law in that place. He spoke to her savagely as they came, and I thought she answered him back. Anyway, a sudden snarl showed on MacTavert's face, and he caught her roughly by the arm, only to pull himself together at once and assume his oily manner as he reached our table.

"This is Colette, sir," he said.

"Splendid!" said Jim lazily. "I ordered whisky, barman," he added.

MacTavert swung round.

"Who are you calling barman?" he snarled. "I'm the owner."

"Are you?" drawled Jim. "How fearfully jolly! But it doesn't alter the fact that I ordered whisky."

The veins stood out on MacTavert's neck like whipcord, and his face turned to an ugly red. There was no mistaking the utter contempt in Jim's voice, and MacTavert was not accustomed to contempt. But he found, as others had found before him, that there was something about this tall perfectly dressed individual, with his quite unnecessary eyeglass, which lent force to the old saying about discretion being the better part of valour; and he swung on his heel and slouched over to the bar, while Colette sat down and Jim laughed.

"He wanted me to make you order champagne," she said, "and I wouldn't. Oh, I am so thankful you've come. It terrifies me, this place – more and more every moment."

With a scowl on his face, MacTavert banged down the whisky.

"Four dollars," he grunted.

"Think again," said Jim quietly. "I'm not buying your beastly saloon: merely two glasses of whisky."

"If you don't like the price you can clear out," snarled MacTavert.

"I shall clear out exactly when I please," returned Jim. "In the meantime, there's a dollar for the whisky. And if you don't like the price you can take your poison away and throw it down the sink."

Once again MacTavert retired muttering, with the dollar bill in his great mottled hand. He was being beaten all along the line, and he knew it. He was up against something he couldn't understand – something that left him vaguely frightened, though no power on earth would have made him admit it.

Drunken sailors, mere strength in any form, he had coped with successfully all his life. But in Jim he had encountered something new; and, as with most ill-educated men, anything new made him uneasy. He relapsed into dark mutterings behind his bar, assuring himself with frequent repetition that if he had any further cheek from this toff he would throw him into the street.

In the meantime the toff was smiling across the table at a very frightened girl into whose face the colour was slowly coming back.

"Now," he said quietly, "what we want to know is how you came into this unpleasant place. After that, we must see how we can get you out."

"You'll think me a fool when I tell you," she whispered miserably.

"We've all of us made idiots of ourselves at one time or another," Jim assured her. "Tell me, Colette: you're not French, are you, like your name?"

The girl laughed. "No, I'm English." Her voice faltered for a moment. "I come from Sussex; from a little village lying under the South Downs."

Jim leant across the table.

"Steady," he said. "Don't cry. I want to talk to you about that little village. I want to find out how you came to leave it."

Then, little by little, we heard the whole pitiful tale. She had run away from home – she who was called Colette. It was dull, and a gentleman had assured her that she would be able to earn big money in London. On the stage, he said – pretty clothes and jewels, and lots of dancing and amusement. So she had stolen out of the house one night, and gone up to London to an address he had told her. She had never seen her mother and father again – and for a time, as she came to that part of her story, she fell silent.

The address in London to which she had gone so hopefully turned out to be a theatrical agency. There an oily gentleman took stock of her and offered her a job with a company that was to go on tour in South America. He had assured her that all she required was experience, and that on her return he would get her an engagement at a West End theatre. She swallowed it whole, as hundreds of other girls have swallowed it.

Then came the awakening. The company had played for a week in a fifth-rate hall in Valparaiso, only to find last Saturday night that the manager had decamped with what money there was. They were stranded, practically penniless, in a foreign town, with not a soul to turn to for assistance. The rest we knew already; the woman with the kindly offer of assistance – the woman in MacTavert's pay.

"She seemed so nice," said Colette miserably, "and then I found myself here."

Once again the poor child's eyes filled with tears; she was paying a big price for her one mistake of foolish vanity in England. Jim's eyes were gentle as he looked at her.

"I see," he said quietly, "and I'm thinking it was lucky you saw us today. This sort of place is not for the likes of you.

"And now," he continued cheerfully, "the only thing that remains is to get you away. I don't think we'll bother about your box and things tonight. I'll fix up about them tomorrow morning. We'll just walk out, and I'll find you a room at some hotel."

He smiled as he saw the look of amazed hope on the girl's face – a look which faded almost as quickly as it had come.

"Well, what's troubling you now?" he said.

"I can't," she cried. "It's wonderful of you to have thought of it – but I can't."

"Why not?" His voice was a little stern.

"There was a missionary here last night," she said. "He took one of the girls away, and that brute MacTavert got two men he keeps here, and they threw him into the docks and nearly drowned him."

"And you're afraid they will do that to me?"

She nodded. "I couldn't have you hurt for me," she answered. "I'm not worth it."

Jim was polishing his eyeglass, which had suddenly become a bit misty.

"Thank you," he said quietly after a while. "But you needn't worry, I promise you. Somehow or other I don't think MacTavert and his pals will throw me or Dick into any dock. If they do," he went on with a sudden grin, "I'll guarantee that they will come in with us."

He pushed back his chair and rose to his feet.

"Come along; we'll go now."

He led the way towards the door, and after a moment's hesitation the girl followed him. They had got halfway when MacTavert saw them. With a shout of anger he rushed out from behind the bar, and reached the door just ahead of Jim.

"Where are you taking that gel to?" he demanded, barring the way.

Instantly a silence settled on the room; everyone craned forward to see what was going to happen. Colette, her breath coming in little frightened gasps, cowered close to me, while her eyes were fixed on the tall figure of Jim.

"In England, MacTavert," he remarked – and every word cut like a knife through the room – "in England you would be flogged with the cat for your method of living. Unfortunately, we are not in England, and so I propose to take the law into my own hands. If you don't get out of my way I shall hit you."

MacTavert laughed, or rather he bared his yellow teeth in what was intended to be a grin. At last this man was talking the language that he understood; and MacTavert, to do him justice, was no coward.

"You'll hit me, Percy, will you?" he mimicked. "Sure, you frighten me!"

A burst of laughter went round the room, which died away in a gasp of astonishment. At one moment MacTavert was standing there leering at Jim – the next he had disappeared. Only the drumming of his feet, which stuck out from under a table that he had overturned in his fall indicated his position. Not till the drumming ceased did Jim turn and contemplate the room.

"When he takes interest again," he remarked pleasantly to no one in particular, "you can remind him that I gave him fair warning."

He passed through the door, and we followed, no one lifting a finger to prevent us.

"Easy!" said Jim. "But I think we'll get a move on now. When MacTavert wakes up he won't be full of brotherly love."

We walked quickly away up the street, the girl between us, and as we turned the corner I looked back. As far as I could see the street was deserted, and I breathed more freely. At last we reached a small and respectable-looking hotel, and after a brief survey Jim decided it would do. A room was available, and he engaged it for Colette.

"I'll be round in the morning," he said, cutting short her thanks with a smile. "Until then, you go to bed and sleep."

We watched her go up the stairs before we left. At the top she turned and waved her hand, and Jim waved back.

"Poor kid!" he said as we went out into the street. "Thank heaven we were here, and she saw us!"

He paused suddenly, gripping my arm, and stared across the road.

"Under that tree, Dick," he whispered. "Do you see anything?"

It seemed to me there was a shadow on the path such as a man might throw. But when we got there, there was nothing. The road was deserted, and at last we turned and retraced our steps towards our own hotel.

It was eleven o'clock next morning when we returned to the hotel where we had left Colette – and found she had gone.

The clerk, in the intervals of picking his teeth, informed us that a message had come round for her to the effect that the gentleman with the eyeglass wished her to come at once to his hotel, the Grand, and she had gone. Apparently her bill had been paid, and he could tell us nothing more. A car had been waiting and she had got in.

"What a fool I was, Dick!" Jim snapped when we were standing in the sunny street outside the hotel. "MacTavert has got her back."

"What about going to the police?" I suggested.

"Man, we've got no proof," he cried. "And even if we had, the police in a place like this are no more use than a sick headache. We've got to handle this thing ourselves, Dick. Are you game?"

"Of course," I said briefly. "What's the first move?"

"A further conversation with MacTavert," he remarked. "And at once."

The dancing saloon was empty as we turned into it. The reek of stale smoke and spirits was worse than the night before, but it was evidently too early for the crowd to arrive.

"So much the better," said Jim grimly. "It gives us a clear field."

He gave a shout of "Bar!" and after a moment or two MacTavert's evil face appeared through a door. He stared at us for a time in silence, then pressed an electric bell twice.

"This bar don't open till midday," he remarked at length.

"That's very fortunate," said Jim placidly. "It gives us an hour to break it up in. How is the face this morning?"

"Get out of it!" roared MacTavert.

"Certainly," answered Jim. "The instant that you produce Colette I shall be delighted to go."

But the scoundrel wasn't going to give himself away.

"So you've lost her, have you?" he sneered. "She fooled you nicely last night, didn't she?"

He was leaning over the bar, shaking with laughter.

"You dear little mother's innocent, with your little pane of glass in your eye! I admit you can hit, but you've a lot to learn yet, Percy. Sling him out, boys," he snarled suddenly.

I swung round to see two men creeping on Jim from behind – two men who had entered noiselessly while MacTavert was talking. They were great powerful brutes, in better condition than MacTavert, and they thought they had a soft thing on. Slinging out a toff with an eyeglass was just pure pleasure – better even than half-drowning a missionary.

It was then I discovered what a wonderful weapon a bottle of French vermouth can be if used skilfully. So did the leading tough. He crashed like a log, with vermouth dripping from his head, and Jim returned the broken bottle to MacTavert.

"A poor fighter," he murmured placidly, though his eyes were very bright and watchful. "Is your other friend going to sling me out?"

But the second man showed no signs of attempting anything of the sort. He was muttering to MacTavert behind the bar, and suddenly the latter began to grin.

"There's something up, Jim," I whispered, and he nodded without speaking.

"Well, Percy," said MacTavert, at length, "we've kind of come to the conclusion that that girl must be your sister. So out of the kindness of my heart I guess you may take her – if you can. She is through that door there and up the stairs. The room on the right is hers. As I say, you may take her if you can."

The leer had deepened on his face, and Jim was watching him narrowly.

"Not afraid, are you?" sneered MacTavert. "I'll come with you and show you the way."

He slouched over to the door, and we followed him. Jim had his hand in his pocket, and I could see the outline of his gun, but if MacTavert saw it he gave no sign. He led the way up the stairs, and paused at the top, waiting for us.

It was then I noticed that the other man had left the bar. It was empty save for the unconscious scoundrel on the floor.

"Here's the room," remarked MacTavert, flinging open the door and leading the way in.

"You brute!" roared Jim as we saw the terrified girl. She was lashed to a chair and gagged. In an instant he was beside her, undoing the rope, and Colette was free.

"Cover him, Dick!" he ordered briefly, and my gun went into MacTavert's waistcoat. His great coarse face was within a few inches of mine, but it was the look of triumph in his eyes that warned me of the trap. He was staring at something over my shoulder, and suddenly he gave a great shout of "Now!"

I swung round, like the fool I was, and the next moment he had knocked my revolver away, and his hands were round my throat. Out of the corner of my eye I saw Jim fighting desperately with two men who had sprung through the door, but it wasn't there that the trap lay; it wasn't that which had caused the sudden shout of "Now!"

Coming towards the window from the outside along a flat piece of roof was the man who had been talking to MacTavert downstairs. He had a revolver in his hand, and he was covering Jim through the window – Jim, who was all unconscious of the danger. I strove to warn him, but MacTavert had got my throat, and it was all I could do to hold my own. The triumph deepened in MacTavert's eyes.

The two men were being flung all over the place by Jim, but they hung on and steadily manoeuvred him nearer and nearer to the window. He had his back towards it, and once the man outside raised his revolver, only to drop it again as the three of them spun round, spoiling his shot.

But it couldn't last long, and I put forth one supreme effort to get the better of MacTavert. We crashed, both of us rolling over and over on the floor. That was why I didn't see the actual deed by which Colette saved our lives. All I knew was that suddenly we were fighting in darkness, MacTavert and I. I heard dimly the crashing of the window, and the splintering of wooden shutters. Then two shots rang out quickly, and the room was light again.

Instinctively MacTavert and I loosened our hold on one another, and got dazedly to our feet. Save for our heavy breathing and a sob from that wonderful girl, there was silence in the room.

"She closed those wooden shutters," said Jim at length, and his voice was a little dazed. "She closed those wooden shutters, and put her arm where the bar ought to be that holds them. She hadn't time, I guess, for the bar. And he broke her arm for her."

He looked at the man who had done it – the man who had smashed through the shutters and fired at him. He was lying motionless on his face. He looked at Colette, and she had fainted. Then he looked at MacTavert, and his face was terrible to see.

"Get out!" snarled Jim to the two men whom he had been fighting. He slipped his own revolver back in his pocket. "Get out – or I might shoot you, as I shot him."

The men slunk out, leaving MacTavert alone. For a moment Jim stared at him, and his eyes were hard and merciless. Then without a word he sprang on him, and MacTavert gave a hoarse cry for help. But there was no one to answer it, and Jim laughed gently.

He could have done it by himself, for MacTavert was like a child in his hands. But since I was there to help him it took less time. We lashed him to the bed face down.

"The cat is the proper weapon for MacTavert," Jim remarked, "as I think I told you last night. But since I haven't got one a leather strap must do instead."

He flogged MacTavert with his leather belt till MacTavert fainted, even as Colette had fainted. Then, with the tenderness of a woman, he picked the girl up in his arms and carried her down the stairs to the saloon below. It was still empty, and we chartered a passing cab and got in. It was on the way to a doctor that Colette opened her eyes and looked at him.

"He didn't hurt you?" she whispered.

We fixed up a passage for her, and as I said before she has two little Colettes of her own now. But I wonder if she realises...

CHAPTER 5

The Fight at Bull Mine Creek

We first heard the rumour at Sydney three months later, from a man in our hotel. Two nights later he confirmed it: gold had been found at a place called Bull Mine Creek. The wildest stories were flying round: it was going to be a second Klondyke.

There was gold in the river, masses of it; and since easily worked placers are nearly all exhausted, thousands of the old-time miners arrived in force. Deep placer deposits, requiring shaft sinking and capital, are today the source of almost all the gold in the world, and the industry is a highly organised affair. The wild rushes of the last century are things of the past, though occasionally they still occur. Bull Mine Creek was one of them.

Exactly why Jim and I went there I don't know. Novelty, perhaps – a new experience; and new experiences were life to him. We didn't much mind if we made a fortune or not, though we should neither have refused. Incidentally we didn't, and what we did net after expenses had been paid, we handed over to One-eyed Mike, an old scoundrel who had lost his left eye in circumstances we never fully got to the bottom of. He was a remarkable character, was Mike. His nationality varied according to his company. With us he was English, and he appeared to have been in every mining rush during the last thirty years. I think he robbed us right and left, though, like the Chinese servant, he took care that nobody else did. And he knew everything there was to know about the game.

He talked about sluice-boxes and riffles in the intervals of telling the most lurid stories I have ever listened to, and for six weeks we camped out by our claim some fifteen miles from the town of Bull Mine Creek.

The town consisted of a few shanties, a store and the hotel. Before the rush it must have been a fairly pleasant little place; but within a week of the boom gambling saloons opened, and the place was invaded by a horde of blackguards whose sole aim in life was to see that the miner and his gold were soon parted. In many cases it wasn't a difficult proposition.

It was One-eyed Mike who insisted on going down to the town for Christmas, and since he had behaved for some weeks we felt he deserved a respite. So Jim gave him his share up to date, and on Christmas Eve we all drove into Bull Mine Creek.

Outside the door of the hotel was a buggy drawn by two fine Arabs, around which stood a ring of loungers. The horses were tied up to the rail of the veranda, and Jim glanced at them as we drove past.

"A nice pair of cattle," he remarked. "I wonder whom they belong to."

The next moment our own horse stopped suddenly, and then gave a sudden plunge forward. She was not used to having her head nearly pulled off unexpectedly, and Jim was certainly not accustomed to treat an animal in such a way. I looked at him, and the expression on his face amazed me. It also decided me against any comment.

Instead, I looked back and made a further inspection of the owner of the two Arabs, whose sudden appearance had so upset my companion. He was a tall good-looking man of about thirty. He had a small fair moustache, and was rather of the pink and white type. So much I saw before we turned the corner and were out of sight. My last glimpse of him was leading his two horses towards the back of the hotel.

Jim drove on in silence to the shanty where we were putting up. He was frowning thoughtfully, and underneath the beard which he had allowed to grow during the past two months his mouth was set in a straight line. But he said nothing, and only nodded curtly at One-eyed Mike's hope that we would raise the roof with him that night.

"Did you see that fellow, Dick?" said Jim at length.

"I did," I answered. "Who is he?"

Jim smiled a little grimly.

"He is John James Hildebrand, fifteenth Marquis of Sussex, the eldest son of the Duke of Plumpton."

"All that, is he?" I said. "One rather wonders what he is doing at Bull Mine Creek."

"One does," agreed Jim. "Excessively so."

With that he swung on his heel, and I saw him no more for some hours. I wrote two or three letters, and then strolled along the dusty road to the hotel. The place was filling up with the crowd who had come in for Christmas, and the first man I saw was One-eyed Mike. He beckoned to me joyously and I went over to his table.

"There's going to be some fun here tonight, boy!" he cried as I sat down. "There's a dude that calls himself Hildebrand wandering around, and the boys are just crazy to know him better. They want to know if he's real."

So the fifteenth Marquis of Sussex had decided not to advertise his identity.

"What's he doing here, Mike?" I asked.

"Come out to look at some property he's got, so he told the boss here. Taken a room, and wants his dinner served upstairs." Mike began to chuckle again. "Look out; here he is."

John James Hildebrand had just entered the room from the other end, and I watched him curiously. Following close at his heels came half a dozen miners, all gazing at him in rapt awe and admiration. The baiting of John James had begun in earnest.

He halted by the bar, and the miners instantly came to a standstill.

"Boys," shouted the leader, "let us have silence! Mr Hildebrand is about to consume some liquid refreshment."

A dead silence settled on the room, and I wondered how he was going to take it.

"Quite right," he remarked, with a faint, rather pleasant drawl. "Which is why I don't ask you to join me. Six of you, all drinking, would fairly put the lid on."

The leader roared with laughter. Obviously John James had the right stuff in him.

"I'm dashed if you drink alone, Mr Hildebrand," cried the leader. "You drink with me right here."

He shouted for a round, and they formed up on each side of John James.

"I'm not so certain that you are going to have your fun, Mike," I remarked, when suddenly he stared at the door which had just swung open.

"Holy Moses!" he muttered. "Here's Pete Cornish. I didn't know he was up these parts."

A sudden cessation of conversation took place as the man moved up to the bar. As if he had noticed it, and attributed it to his sudden entry, a faint smile hovered round his lips. His face was almost bloodless, and a great red scar across his right cheek emphasised the pallor. But the most noticeable feature of the man's face was a pair of very light blue eyes which seemed to stare unwinkingly from under his big forehead. He stooped a little, but even so he measured over six feet; and the depth of his chest betokened his immense strength.

"Steer clear of him, boy," muttered Mike to me. "I haven't seen him for six years, but I guess he hasn't changed. He's spent fifteen years of his life in prison as it is."

But I wasn't paying much attention to Mike. I was watching Pete Cornish. He came to a standstill just behind John James, and for a moment or two stood in silence. It was the miner who had called for drinks who first saw him, and he turned round with a somewhat sickly smile.

"Hullo, Pete!" he said. "Will you join us?"

"I will," answered Cornish quietly. "And who is your friend?"

"Hildebrand," returned the other. "This is Pete Cornish."

"Pleased to meet you, Mr Hildebrand," said Cornish. "And what might you be doing? Prospecting?"

"I've come out to see a property of mine," answered Hildebrand briefly.

The blue eyes never left his face for an instant, even when their owner raised his glass to his lips. There was something baleful in their unblinking intensity. The man never moved; he merely stared until after a while the other fidgeted and turned away. The faintest flicker of a smile appeared on Cornish's lips.

"I seem to recognise your face, Mr Hildebrand," he remarked. "In fact, I am sure I do. And so, you will drink with me."

It was not a question: it was a statement, and Hildebrand flushed slightly.

"Thank you, no," he answered. "I don't want any more at present."

"I said, Mr Hildebrand, that you would drink with me," said the other gently – and I noticed that five of the six miners who had lined up at the bar had slipped quietly away. Only the leader remained, and he was shuffling his feet.

"The guy is all right, Pete," he muttered awkwardly. "Guess he may not have the head for our whisky."

The blue eyes turned to the last speaker.

"I'm not quite clear how you come into this matter," remarked Cornish.

The miner turned and stammered out something, but Cornish simply ignored his existence.

"Now, Mr Hildebrand, you will drink a little toast with me," he continued.

"I have already said that I will not have another, thank you," returned the other icily. "I drink when I like, and with whom I like."

He nodded briefly and turned to leave the bar. But before he had taken two steps Cornish had stretched out a hand and caught him by the arm.

"Will you kindly leave go of my arm?" said Hildebrand quietly, though two ugly red spots had appeared on his face.

"When you have drunk my toast, Mr Hildebrand; not before."

For a moment John James, fifteenth Marquis of Sussex, stood very still. He was no fool, and he knew that if it came to a scrap he might with luck last exactly one second. At the same time he came of a stock to whom fear was unknown.

"And what is your toast?" he asked at length.

"Damnation to the English – especially their aristocracy," answered the other mildly. "Your glass, Mr Hildebrand."

The Marquis of Sussex smiled faintly, as he took the glass in his right hand. Then – it was done in one movement – the heavy glass broke in pieces on Cornish's face. He staggered back a step, and without undue hurry, but also without undue pause, John James Hildebrand left the room. For a moment or two I expected Cornish to rush after him, but he didn't. He stood in the centre of the room wiping the whisky from his face. Then, without a word, he too turned and left the bar.

It was the miner by the counter who broke the silence.

"Good for the youngster!" he cried. "But, my word, boys, Pete will kill him for that."

The murmur of assent was stilled by the sudden reappearance of Hildebrand.

"Oh! he's gone, has he?" he said cheerfully. "It struck me after I got upstairs that I had left a bit quickly, and that he might think I was afraid of him. But you see, gentlemen – my wife is with me, and one doesn't want to get mixed up in a scrap."

The miner at the counter took a step forward.

"See here, Mr Hildebrand," he said earnestly, "you've proved yourself, and I want to apologise here and now for ragging you. But get away out of this. I know Pete Cornish, and I tell you straight he'll pretty near kill you for bunging that glass in his face. Get away now – with your wife. Them greys of yours are good for another fifty miles. We'll get you into your trap, won't we, boys?"

Hildebrand gave a quick smile.

"I thank you, gentlemen," he said quietly. "But if you imagine that my wife and I are going a fifty miles' drive, or fifty yards, because some renegade Irishman gets gay, you misunderstand the situation. And while I am at it I must apologise for my deceit. I'm really Lord Sussex. Hildebrand is a sort of family name."

With another smile he was gone, and a sort of sigh went round the room.

"I don't know nothing about Sussex – nor family names," One-eyed Mike remarked. "But what I do know is that there's going to be dirty work here tonight, and I guess he's going to be the dirt."

I found Jim at the shanty when I got back. He glanced up as I came in, and dropped his month-old newspaper on the floor.

"Anything doing?" he asked.

"Quite a lot," I answered. "Your friend Hildebrand has distinguished himself."

He listened while I told him what had occurred, and a faint look of surprise crossed his face.

"I didn't know he had it in him," he remarked thoughtfully. "In fact, I have always regarded him as no more than his father's eldest son, who would in time become a duke."

"What of it?" I said. "Why the sarcasm?"

"Nothing that I care to go into," he answered. "It's an old story, anyway; but seeing him unexpectedly this evening brought it back – that's all."

"Well, there is every possibility of trouble tonight," I said. "That man Cornish is quite the ugliest-looking customer I've ever seen, and I didn't like the absolute silence in which he left."

Jim shrugged his shoulders.

"John James must fight his own battles."

"He seems quite capable of it," I answered shortly. "But I wish his wife weren't there."

"His wife?" said Jim very slowly. "His wife, did you say? Ruth – at that hotel? Good heavens, man! She can't be."

Jim was pacing up and down the room, frowning deeply. Now and then he paused and stared out of the window.

Already some of the boys had begun their celebrations, and occasional shouts came from the street outside.

"The fellow must be mad!" exploded Jim suddenly. "Confound it, has he left his nurse in England?"

"It's not the boys I'm worried about, Jim," I said gravely. "It's Cornish who frightens me."

Jim laughed contemptuously.

"You've got Cornish on the brain, Dick."

As he spoke the door was flung open and One-eyed Mike came in. He had been running and he spoke in gasps.

"Cornish!" he cried. "Pete Cornish! He's raving mad up in the hotel. He's got that Lord fellow and his wife, and he's doing trick-firing with a couple of revolvers."

As he finished I realised we were alone: Jim was racing towards the hotel.

I heard six shots ring out like bullets from a machine-gun as I followed Jim.

It was an amazing scene. Huddled in small groups sat some twenty miners, looking very sober. In the centre of the room swung a smoking naphtha lamp. Underneath it stood Pete Cornish, holding a girl whose look of frozen horror failed to hide her loveliness.

Seated on a chair against the wall was the fifteenth Marquis of Sussex, and like a halo round his head there was a row of holes in the wall. As Mike said, Pete Cornish was trick-firing.

The man on the chair was sitting bolt upright, while his knuckles gleamed like ivory where his hands gripped the seat. His face was white, but with rage – not fear.

"Don't move, my darling," said Cornish with an ugly snarl. "You might spoil my aim. And that would be a dreadful thing for your dear husband, wouldn't it?"

Again the six shots rang out, and the wood round the seated man's head splintered anew. The girl moaned piteously, and her husband stirred in his chair.

"My other gun," said Cornish thoughtfully, and a horrible-looking brute came forward with a freshly loaded six-shooter. And at that John James Hildebrand sprang. It was his only chance, but it was pitiful to watch. As well might a Pekinese spring at a bull-terrier.

He tried to get home with his fist – and Cornish hit him once, straight in the face. The poor blighter pitched forward and lay still.

"I still want my gun," said Cornish thoughtfully.

As he spoke a shot rang out. The man who was holding the revolver yelled, and Jim laughed gently. Slowly Cornish's blue eyes came round and fastened on him; and for a moment or two there was silence – broken at length by a gasping cry of "Jim!" from the girl.

"Did you fire that shot?" asked Cornish softly, dropping the girl and taking a step forward.

"I did," answered Jim, equally softly. "And I would suggest your standing very still, because I'm now going to fire five more. Stand away, Ruth" – but the girl was on her knees beside her husband.

The five shots cut away a strip from Cornish's shirt, and they sounded almost continuous so incredibly quickly were they fired.

"I have also another gun," drawled Jim, "so that any attempt to pick up your own would be a little unwise. Dick, would you get it?"

Cornish never moved a muscle. The scar on his face showed red and angry, but the eyes went on staring at Jim.

"Quite passable shooting," he said at length. "And what do you propose should be the next move? Or do we stand like this all night?"

"We do not," answered Jim. "I have been informed of the toast you suggested to Lord Sussex, and it fails to appeal to me. So having given you a little of your own medicine in the shooting line, we will now try the second form of exercise. We will fight here and now to a finish with our fists."

A sudden triumphant gleam came into Cornish's eyes, and an audible gasp ran round the room. Was this fellow with an eyeglass completely insane? But only One-eyed Mike said anything, and he was nearly frantic.

"Don't do it," he whispered to Jim. "He's been a professional, and he's a slaughterer, even with gloves."

But Jim paid no attention. He was peeling off his shirt and giving me instructions.

"If he fights fair, Dick, do nothing. But if any of his pals get gay, I rely on you."

For a moment he glanced across the room to where the girl sat crouched on the floor with her unconscious husband's head pillowed on her lap, and he smiled whimsically.

"I've got over it now," he said, "but seven years ago I thought my world had finished when she turned me down for him. But he's a good boy, Dick, and if Cornish knocks me out – well, again I rely on you."

Then he stepped into the circle of light thrown by the naphtha lamp.

Men still talk about that fight on Christmas Eve in the hotel at Bull Mine Creek. Word had flashed round the camp like lightning that a man was taking on Pete Cornish, bare fists, to a finish, and men came pouring in till the room was crammed almost to suffocation. It was obvious which way their sympathies lay. Not one out of ten knew Jim, but there wasn't a soul in the room who did not know and hate Pete Cornish. The betting started at five to one on Cornish, for his form was known; but the odds shortened to threes when Jim, stripped to the waist, was sized up. But there wasn't a soul who wouldn't willingly have lost his money to see Cornish down and out.

There was no time wasted on preliminaries, but one could feel the nerve-gripping tension as the two men faced one another, swaying slightly under the flaring lamp. Cornish, his blue eyes fixed unwinkingly on Jim, was a shade the bigger man of the two. As he crouched a little forward, his huge depth of chest was more than ever apparent, and a feeling of sick anxiety got hold of me. Without doubt he was amazingly powerful, and the look of rage on his face boded ill for Jim.

Then I glanced at Jim, and felt better. In my own mind I sized up the position, to find later that it was exactly how Jim had sized it up himself. Cornish was the stronger man of the two, and probably the better boxer; but he was not in such good condition.

They closed, and a kind of sigh went round. Smack, smack and they were away again, with a jolting punch on Jim's jaw as Cornish's contribution, and a heavy body blow which made Cornish draw breath with a hiss. It was not a spectacular punch, but as Jim said to me afterwards, it probably won him the fight, for it touched up Cornish's wind, and there lay his weakness. Inside a minute a sullen-looking purple patch was showing on his ribs.

But there was a long way to go yet, and a punishing way. Cornish was no fool; he knew his weakness, and started to force the fighting. A quick decision was his best hope, and for the next three minutes my heart was in my mouth. Savagely, but never wildly, he went for Jim, taking his own punishment without a sound. At least two of his upper cuts, if they had got home, would have ended the fight there and then.

But they didn't. Coolly and warily Jim gave ground, letting the other man follow him round and round the room, and concentrating always on Cornish's body. Twice, three times he landed heavy punishing blows, and was away before the other had time to counter.

The room was deadly silent. The patter of their feet was the only sound; that, and what was music to me – Cornish's laboured breathing. Then suddenly an angry roar burst out.

"Too low, Cornish! Foul!"

With a snarl Cornish sprang back, but Jim was smiling now. It was an attempted foul right enough, but Jim countered just in time, and then changed his tactics. Rightly he guessed that it was the other man's last throw. His breathing was becoming more and more painful. From the defensive he changed to the attack. He gave Cornish not one second's respite; he was here, there and everywhere, waiting for the opportunity of a knock-out. Twice Cornish hit him, but he was weakening perceptibly. His blue eyes still stared at Jim, but he was getting slower and slower, while he sucked in air in great wheezing gasps.

Quite suddenly came the end. Jim feinted at his body, and as his guard dropped Jim hit him under the jaw. Feet, body and weight were exactly right. The blow sounded like a billiard ball on a wooden floor. Cornish spun round, his knees sagging under him, and crumpled up on the floor, while Jim stood watching him and rubbing the knuckles of his right hand. For the blow that knocked out Cornish had also broken three of Jim's fingers.

There was one dazed moment while nobody spoke; then pandemonium broke loose. A crowd of miners thronged across to where Jim stood, led by One-eyed Mike, who was nearly speechless.

"Knocked out! Cornish knocked out!" he kept on saying over and over again. "And he's my pardner, you sons of a gun – don't you forget it!"

With a faint smile on his battered face Jim pushed through to where his clothes lay.

"Tell 'em to come to our shanty," he muttered to me. "They can't stop here."

With that he was gone, and I crossed the room to Lord Sussex and his wife. He was conscious again, but it was the girl I was looking at. I had to deliver my message three times before she took it in.

We found Jim trying to cut the wire of a champagne bottle. The Marchioness of Sussex walked straight up to him.

"I hardly know you, Jim," she said, a little tremulously, "without your eyeglass."

Jim grinned. "I'm afraid we shall have to dispense with that for a day or two."

"Good heavens!" shouted John James Hildebrand. "It's Jim Maitland!"

"Bright boy!" said his wife, and it struck me she wasn't quite at her ease.

"I only came to when you were fighting," he went on, "and I never recognised you."

Then he too dried up a little awkwardly.

"By Gad, old man," he said steadily, after a moment, "I feel it horribly, that I couldn't fight my own battles for myself. It was fine of you to take that brute on – fine!"

Jim poured out the champagne.

"I don't profess that I'd have done it five years ago, or even tonight if Ruth hadn't been there," he remarked quietly.

Then he smiled suddenly.

"Yes, I would. Your going for him was a sight better than my show. We can't all be made big, old chap."

He held out his sound hand.

"John," he said, "shake. I haven't loved you much for the past seven years. In fact I haven't loved you at all. I thought lots of things at the time. But the years have healed, and – " He turned to the girl. "Is it well with you, Ruth?"

"Yes," she answered. "My dear, I'm sorry. But what annoyed me was that you thought I married John just because he would be a duke one day."

Jim nodded thoughtfully.

"I was a fool," he said quietly. "Still," he added whimsically, "perhaps it was as well. I've had seven good years in the edge of beyond."

"You're very rude," laughed the girl. "We'll have to find you a wife now, Jim."

"You preferred your blessed old John James," Jim said, "and the other thinks I'm a cur. She told me so – in Tampico."

"Then she must be mad," said Ruth indignantly. "Where is she now, Jim?"

"In England somewhere."

"Then come and look for her."

Jim laughed. "I don't know about that, but if I come back I'll spend a few days at the ancestral seat if you'll have me."

"If you don't," cried John James, "you'll have to fight me, my boy."

"You'll come, Jim," his wife repeated. "And Mr Leyton too."

"Shall we go back to England, Dick?" he said.

"The one sure thing," I remarked, "is that if we decide to, we shan't."

"You see our habits, Ruth," he said. "We're dreadful people to have about the house. Anyway I don't know what you think, Dick, but we might take the first step on the journey in the near future. Gold mining at a hundred and ten in the shade is an overrated amusement."

And at that we left it.

CHAPTER 6

Pete Cornish's Revenge

That evening at Bull Mine Creek was the first time that the curtain had been lifted on Jim's past. Even to me he had never talked. Jim wasn't made that way. But as he wished Lady Sussex a merry Christmas next morning I couldn't help wondering what difference it would have made to him if she had become Mrs Maitland...

We saw them off from the hotel, and stood in the road watching till the dust from their buggy had died away in the distance. Then we started to stroll back to our shanty. Jim started a smile – but it didn't last.

"Whew!" he cried. "Don't let me laugh again. It hurts. Mr Pete Cornish has got what you might describe as a fairly useful punch behind him."

"Once or twice last night, Jim, I thought he'd got you."

Jim nodded briefly.

"So did I. Especially in that first minute. I don't mind telling you, Dick, that if that first smack on my jaw had been half an inch lower, it would have been a knock-out. His poor condition did the trick."

We paused at the door of our shanty as One-eyed Mike came down the steps to meet us. A broad smile adorned his face.

"A merry Christmas, boys!" he cried, and then he went into a fit of chuckling. "To think of it: Pete Cornish knocked out with bare fists inside ten minutes! I wouldn't have believed it possible. I just wouldn't have believed it possible. I'd give every penny I possess in the world to see you do it again."

"You don't seem particularly fond of him, Mike," said Jim, as he went indoors.

"Fond of him!" snarled the other. "Eight years ago he swindled me out of the best claim I ever had; and when I taxed him with it, he and two of his pals waylaid me. That's where I lost this eye."

"A cheerful sort of customer," said Jim thoughtfully. "Well, you got a bit of your own back last night. Now that you're here, Mike, we might go into business. Dick and I are going back to England – perhaps…"

"Quitting?" There was genuine regret in One-eyed Mike's voice. "Boys, that's too bad. I guess you've got a real good claim up there."

"It's yours, Mike," said Jim.

Speechless surprise showed in the one eye, and Mike's voice was a little husky as he answered.

"I don't know what to say, sir," he remarked at length. "Cornish didn't tap you on the head or anything last night?"

Jim laughed. "No, we're quite sane, Mike. But we're going back to look for somebody."

"I hope you find her," said Mike, and then he strolled to the window and stood staring out down the dusty street.

"Bud Sandford's up early this morning," he observed presently. "Moreover, pards, he's coming here unless I'm greatly mistook."

The next moment Sandford entered. He held no official Government position, though his power was far greater than if he had. By common consent he had been elected boss, sheriff and general settler of disputes, and what he said at Bull Mine Creek went. He was about fifty, with shrewd grey eyes and a reputation for fairness which was just what was wanted in such a community.

"Morning, Bud," said Jim. "Take a seat."

Bud Sandford lit a cigar.

"Morning," he said. "How's the face?"

Jim grinned. "It wants a week's rest, and it'll grow again."

Bud gazed out of the window.

"I saw your scrap last night," he remarked, "and lost a tenner. I'd willingly have lost two. I suppose you know it was a quarter of an hour before Cornish sat up and took notice?"

"As long as that?" said Jim. "I must have hit him harder than I thought."

"It's not to talk about that that I came around, though," Bud went on. "It was to find out what you propose doing in the near future."

Jim looked a trifle surprised.

"I and my pal here are quitting, and our claim passes to Mike," he said at length.

Bud grunted thoughtfully.

"When are you quitting?"

"Today or tomorrow," answered Jim. "We haven't really thought about it."

"I guess I'd feel happier if you could make it today," said Bud.

"You seem almighty keen to be rid of us, Bud," said Jim. "What's the idea?"

Once again Bud's eyes travelled to the window.

"Just this, boy," he said. "Another twenty-four hours' rest, and the effect of that blow on Pete Cornish's jaw will be wearing off, but the effect on his mind will be wearing in. Do you follow me?"

"Not frightfully clearly, Bud," remarked Jim ominously. "I fail to see any relation between Pete Cornish's jaw and my future plans."

Bud Sandford's grey eyes twinkled.

"I was afraid you mightn't," he confessed, "though it seems powerful clear to me. Look here, son," he went on, "this is how the land lies. You beat Pete Cornish last night in fair fight. If you fought him again, fair, you'd do it again. But next time you won't fight fair – because Pete won't let you. Now you've beaten him he'll stop at nothing till he's got his own back, and you won't cut much ice against a man with a rifle, hiding up an alley-way and shooting you in the back. That's what Pete Cornish will do, or something like it, unless you pass out of the picture while he's still holding a raw rump steak to his jaw."

Jim smiled.

"It's very good of you, Bud," he remarked quietly. "I'd just love to take your advice. But I've come to the conclusion that I don't like travelling on Christmas Day."

"Fiddlesticks!" Bud remarked. "You'll be a fool if you stay in Bull Mine Creek until tomorrow."

"Or maybe the day after," murmured Jim. "We've got to do a bit of business, Bud: transferring our claim to Mike."

Bud rose and flung his cigar through the window.

"If I hadn't come around," he remarked, "you might have gone today. But I can promise you one thing, boy: if we can get the smallest shadow of proof we'll hang him the same time as we bury you. And even if we can't, we'll hang him, I think. Pete Cornish has gone on too long."

The door closed behind him, only to open again as he popped his head round. "You'd better think out a good epitaph," he said genially. "Something snappy and original. The last one I made up won't apply, though it's good:

> *Here lies Bill Soames, a funny sort of joker;*
> *Who held four aces, when he didn't deal at poker.*"

For the rest of Christmas Day nothing happened to justify Bud's forebodings. We squared up our few belongings and carried out the formalities for re-registering our claim in One-eyed Mike's name. If only Sandford had not come butting in, we should have cleared off that evening in the cool. As it was, we didn't.

We saw no signs of Cornish that day. In the hotel we gathered that he was lying up somewhere paying earnest attention to his jaw. We also gathered that the general feeling of the community agreed with Bud.

"Pete Cornish ain't finished yet, pard," said one, "and never will be till some public benefactor kills him. And that guy whose hand you shot last night is almost as bad – Yellow Sam."

Jim smiled.

"Very well, then," he said, "I guess I'd better keep the old head cool."

"You weren't here last night when he came to," the first speaker went on. "I was – and I watched him. He sat up, and stared around for a moment or two as if he didn't realise what had happened. Then he remembered. Them eyes of his – well, a sort of film came over them; and then they cleared, and he looked quite slowly and carefully all round the room. Reckon he was looking for you, but you'd gone. He never spoke; he just got up and walked out into the street – and there was a look on his face such as I've never seen on any living man, and hope I never shall again. I tell you straight," his voice was very quiet and serious, "if he could get you into his power by some dirty trick – heaven help you!"

There was a growl of assent, and he lifted his glass and nodded to Jim:

"Well," he said, "here's fortune, pard. All I say to you is: Keep your gun handy as you drive over Lone Gully tomorrow. There's fifteen miles there where lots of things might happen."

It was as we were returning to our shanty that I happened to glance up at a house we were passing. What I saw quite distinctly was a pair of light-blue eyes staring at us with a look of such hatred that I paused in spite of myself. Then the eyes disappeared, and I walked on at Jim's side. But I couldn't help wishing, as I blew out my candle that night, that a railway line had extended to Bull Mine Creek. The prospect of driving over Lone Gully failed to appeal to me.

We were away by four next morning. One-eyed Mike – not at his best at that hour – was there to see us off. Poor blighter! he little knew that it was the last time he was to see that sun rise: that before the end of the day he was to be shot without mercy by that cold-blooded murderer, Cornish. Rough honest sportsman, he came to save our lives, and lost his own. But perhaps he knows that it wasn't altogether in vain: perhaps he knows that his murderer followed him not long after.

I'm getting on too fast. But sometimes even now I dream of that half-hour when death stared us in the face at the old mine-shaft in Lone Gully, and I wake dripping with sweat. What Jim must have gone through is beyond my comprehension: in fact, he once confessed to me that if he ever had a nightmare it was always the same. He dreams that his hand – the one he had hurt the preceding night – failed him as he swung for over a minute, with certain death as the result if he let go.

But, as I said, I'm getting on too fast.

Our idea as we left Bull Mine Creek was to push on till about ten o'clock, and then to call a halt until four. We reckoned on reaching the beginning of the deserted stretch known as Lone Gully in the morning, and getting across it in the evening. The next day would see us on the railway. So we calculated, as we drove steadily along the flat dusty road.

The sun was not too powerful, and Jim's jaw had recovered enough to allow him to sing. The air was like wine, and after a while I forgot Pete Cornish. There had been no sign of him or his pal that morning, and every mile between us and Bull Mine Creek seemed to lessen the likelihood of trouble.

Half-past nine found us at the place where we had decided to stop for the midday halt, and it was none too soon. Already the sun was uncomfortably hot, and the buggy we were driving would not have won a prize for springing.

"Grub first," said Jim, "and then a little sleep. And perhaps we might take it in turns to watch."

We scanned the country in the direction from which we had come, but there was no sign of movement. The shimmering heat haze blurred and contorted the ground, but of life there seemed no sign.

"I can't help feeling sorry we've got no rifle," remarked Jim thoughtfully, a little later. "A revolver is all very well in its way, but not much use against a gun. However, I don't believe we're going to have any trouble. They've made a bogy man of Mister Pete Cornish, whereas he's merely a low-down bully."

Sure enough, when we harnessed up again at four, there had been no sign of him. Once, about noon, I thought I saw a little cloud of dust moving two or three miles away, but I had no field-glasses, and it was quite possibly my imagination.

The track began to rise almost at once towards Lone Gully. The place deserved its name. On each side of the road ran a line of low broken hills covered with huge boulders and scrub, while here and there disused sheds and the remains of old furnaces showed the positions of worked-out mines.

But Jim and I were not thinking of derelict mining ventures as the mare picked her leisurely way up the hill. After a while he looked at me thoughtfully.

"I can't say I like it, Dick," he said. "As a place suited for trouble, you couldn't beat this. We're simply two slowly travelling bull's-eyes for any man with a gun lying hidden in that stuff."

Involuntarily I thought of that little cloud of dust. What if my eyes had not deceived me? What if that cloud had been a man, or perhaps two, on horseback, making a detour to get in front of us? The idea was not pleasant. No man bent on lawful business would have travelled by any other track save the one we had come by, or have been likely to travel at all during the heat of the day.

I peered ahead, trying to see some sign of movement, but it was hopeless. An army could have hidden concealed, and I soon gave it up. If my forebodings were correct – well, that man was in front of us by now. Somewhere in the fifteen miles we still had to go he could hide himself, so that it would be absolutely impossible to see him until –

I told Jim what I thought I had seen, and his face grew graver.

"I don't like it, Dick," he said. "And I'll never forgive myself, old man, if anything happens. We should have gone yesterday, and it was only my wretched bravado that prevented it."

We had reached the top of the rise as he spoke, and he whipped up the mare. For the next ten miles the road was level, running almost straight between the two lines of low hills. It would take us an hour and a half to get through to the descent the other side and safety. Jim's revolver lay on the seat beside him, while I held mine in my hand, though in our hearts we knew it was a perfectly useless precaution. A revolver is no good at a hundred yards, and we formed an easy target at two hundred to a man with a rifle.

We had been driving perhaps for a quarter of an hour when suddenly Jim stiffened and looked round over his shoulder.

"There's a horse galloping somewhere, Dick," he muttered.

The next instant we saw it. Away back along the dusty road, a man was following us at full gallop.

"That seems a foolish way of doing the trick," said Jim. "I think we'll dismount for a while, and await this gentleman on foot."

The mare stood nibbling at some short grass by the road while the horseman came nearer. Suddenly Jim gave a surprised exclamation.

"It's One-eyed Mike – or I'll eat my hat!"

Mike it was, and I don't know which was sweating more – he or his horse. He flung himself off his saddle, and his breath was coming in great gasps.

"Pete Cornish and Yellow Sam left Bull Mine Creek at ten this morning," he gasped, "riding all out. Said they were going up North... Started that way... But a kid at the house told me she heard 'em talking last night, and they mentioned Prospect Mine. That's here – not a mile on. Their going North was a blind – they're after you. Get in your trap again, Jim – and gallop. They'll have to make a big round to get here, and maybe you'll get through before them."

We had hardly got into the trap when two shots rang out. The shooters were nowhere to be seen, but they could shoot. I saw Mike's horse crumple up, and the next instant I pitched forward out of my seat. Our mare had taken the second bullet, and in falling had broken both shafts. We scrambled out, bewildered. But it wasn't in Jim's nature to remain undecided for long.

"Run like hares," he cried. "Don't run straight – dodge. Get into the scrub if you can."

Had we been able to do it, all might have been well. Once amongst those rocks and bushes, the advantage of rifle over revolver would have disappeared. But as luck would have it, at the particular spot where we had halted, there was a stretch of about seventy yards of open ground before the protection of the low foothills could be reached. We hadn't gone ten yards before another shot rang out and Mike gave a cry of pain. He had been plugged through the shoulder. Instinctively we stopped to help him.

It was then that we saw Cornish. He had risen from behind a boulder about eighty yards away, and his rifle was still up to his shoulder.

"Put up your hands, or I shall fire again."

His voice was perfectly quiet, without a trace of excitement or anger, and for a moment we hesitated. There was another sharp crack, and once again Mike groaned and staggered. This time it was the other shoulder, and it became increasingly obvious that Pete Cornish with a gun was not a man to be played with. Our hands went up, while Mike stood beside us helpless; and there we waited in a row while he leisurely approached us. He had been joined by Yellow Sam, and they both were holding their rifles ready for an immediate shot.

"Take their guns," ordered Cornish as he came up, and his companion disarmed us.

"And now," he continued almost gently, but with his unwinking eyes fixed on Jim, "we will go for a little walk. Then, Mr Maitland, we will have a little talk. After that – who knows? You will keep your hands above your heads, and Sam and I will be behind you. Will you lead the way, Mr Maitland?"

"Where do you propose we go?" said Jim indifferently.

"To that old mine shaft you see there," answered Cornish, and we started off, Jim leading. A rough disused track marked the way up the hill, and after a few minutes' walking we reached a rotting wooden palisade.

"Straight on, Mr Maitland," came the quiet voice from behind us. "Through the gate, and then to the left. That's right, and now we will stop and have our little talk. Kindly stand there in a row and I will endeavour to entertain you."

His blue eyes, with their strange filmy look, never left Jim's face.

"Possibly you are unacquainted with deep placer mining," he began gently. "You are now standing at the top of one of the deepest shafts in the world. Not the main shaft, but a ventilation shaft. As you will see, there is no lift. But you will also note that this shaft has been used for lowering stores or something of that kind: timber perhaps – but the point is a small one. That pulley attached to the overhead beam, which I have carefully oiled this afternoon, Mr Maitland, is immediately over the centre of the shaft. Moreover, this very long coil of rope over the pulley is clearly intended to lower things to the bottom. Considering how long it is since this mine was used, it seems in astonishingly good condition."

Fascinated, I stared at the rope as the whole plot became clear. Coil after coil of it lay on one side of the shaft, but one end passed over the central pulley and was loosely tied to a stake beside Cornish.

"I hope my intentions are clear," he continued gently. "I shall request you to take hold of the end attached to this post, and then walk to the edge of the shaft. You will then step over the edge, and I shall lower you to the bottom. Shortly afterwards your friend will repeat the performance, after which the rope will be thrown down to keep you company. Of course," his voice was almost regretful, "should the rope prove unequal to the strain, or should it be too short, you will drop. The length of the fall will decide whether you do it successfully or not. Oh! and while I think of it, lest you should doubt my words as to the depth – "

His eyes came round to Mike, who shivered.

"We have met before, I think. Just step forward a little. I don't quite know why you have intruded, but since you have – "

It was over in a second. As calmly as if he was eating his dinner Cornish shot, and Mike spun round and toppled over backwards.

"You cold-blooded murderer!" shouted Jim, springing forward. But Cornish's revolver covered him.

"Just listen," said Cornish gently, and with a sick feeling of helpless rage we stood there waiting. At last it came – a dreadful noise which echoed faintly and then died away.

"I should say nearly a quarter of a minute to reach the bottom," he said mildly. "I always believe in removing all traces of these little affairs – and he's not much loss. So now if you're ready, Mr Maitland…"

"And what if I refuse?" said Jim steadily.

"Then your hands will be lashed behind you, and your feet will be attached to the rope, and you will be lowered head first. Failing that, you will be shot here and now. I give you five seconds to decide."

For a second or two Jim hesitated. Then he stepped forward and took the rope in his hands. He knew as well as I did that Cornish would do what he said, and it seemed the only possibility. If he did reach the bottom in safety there might still be a bare chance of getting out somewhere. At any rate it was the only hope.

"Sorry, Dick," he said. "It's my fault."

He gave me that wonderful careless grin of his, and without another word crossed to the edge of the shaft. Then he stared at Cornish.

"Now, you chicken-hearted coward," he said contemptuously, "carry on."

Cornish showed no sign of resenting the insult: his face was quite expressionless.

"I am quite ready, Mr Maitland," he remarked, and Jim swung off into space. There was not a vestige of hesitation, not a trace of fear, though he told me afterwards that he fully expected Cornish to leave go the rope and let him drop. What was really in Cornish's mind must remain an unsolved enigma. Whether he actually did intend to do exactly what he said, or whether he intended to let the rope slip when Jim was halfway down, will never be known.

Certain it is that quietly and steadily he went on paying out the rope, coil after coil, leaning back to take the weight with his feet braced against the shoring at the edge of the shaft, while I watched fascinated and Yellow Sam covered me with his gun.

Then suddenly came the idea. Old memories of mathematics, perhaps, problems on pulleys done in days gone by. Like a flash it came. The coils beside Cornish were getting fewer and fewer, and it had to be done at once.

"Good Lord! Look there!" I shouted, and Yellow Sam turned for a second. There was an iron bar at my feet, and by sheer luck I hit him in the right place.

Now came the second awful risk – would Cornish let go? His blue eyes were staring at me over his shoulder, but for just that fraction of time which meant life or death he didn't realise what I was going to do. He held on to the rope, and as I sprang at him he straightened up instinctively. And with all my force I pushed him in the back.

It was enough. He was off his balance, and with a fearful curse, still clinging on to the rope, he swung out himself over the shaft.

"Hold on, Jim!" I roared. "Hold on!"

For I saw at once that luck had held – Cornish was a heavier man than Jim. For a perceptible time he hung there swaying, his blue eyes almost frenzied in their animal rage, and the scar on his face a livid purple. Then, slowly but steadily, his weight told, and he began to sink down and down. With every foot he fell Jim came up.

For a while Cornish tried to climb, but he could make no headway. Jim was climbing, too, and getting the double advantage. They passed two hundred odd feet below the level of the ground, and Cornish tried to grab Jim's leg. But he kicked himself free, coming up quicker and quicker as the acceleration increased.

Suddenly I heard his voice shouting, urgently: "Check the rope, Dick! Check it somehow!"

For a moment I couldn't understand his reason, but I scrambled out along the beam to the pulley. I used a piece of wood as a brake, and then I saw Jim's plan. He was still fifty feet below me, swaying dizzily, but as the rope checked with the brake and finally stopped, he got the part of it on Cornish's side of the pulley with one hand. Gradually he got both ropes into that hand – shifting his legs to help the strain. And then with his free hand he got out his clasp-knife.

He opened it with his teeth, and Cornish from the depths below realised what was happening. He started frenziedly shooting up the shaft, heedless now of whether he died or not, provided he got Jim too. But he was swaying too much, and the end was quick. Jim cut the rope on Cornish's side below the place where he had both returns gripped in his other hand – and once again there came that dreadful dull noise which echoed faintly and then died away.

Half a minute later, using the two ends of the rope as one, Jim reached the pulley beam, and scrambled into safety. Then, for the first time in his life, Jim Maitland fainted.

Later on we walked to the next township, with Yellow Sam in front of us carrying our bags. We gave him to the inhabitants with our love, and I believe they hanged him, though the point is not of great importance. The man who had called himself Pete Cornish was more dangerous than twenty Yellow Sams, and in his case the hangman had been saved the trouble.

Who Cornish really was is a mystery, for the man talked and spoke like a gentleman. Some maintained that he was the direct descendant of a famous pirate who had ended his days in Botany Bay, after a career of unbelievable ferocity. Who knows? Whatever may be the truth, the one unforgettable picture of him that lives in my mind is just two staring light blue eyes swinging backwards and forwards and then gradually sinking to the death he had planned for us.

CHAPTER 7

The Madman at Corn Reef Lighthouse

If you lie on the close-clipped turf that stretches between Beachy Head and Birling Gap, not too far from the edge of the white chalk cliffs, you will see below you the lighthouse. It stands out in the sea some two hundred yards from the base of the cliff, and every few seconds, once dusk has fallen, the beam from the revolving light will shine on you and pass on, sweeping over the grey water below. It was a dangerous part of the coast, one time a haunt of smugglers, till the lighthouse made it safe.

There are treacherous currents and shoals; but the worst is when the sea mist comes gently drifting over the Downs and lies like a grey blanket over the sea below. Then that sweeping light is useless, and every two or three minutes there comes from the lighthouse the sound of a maroon, which is answered by the mournful wailing of sirens out to sea, as vessels creep slowly through the fog, which eddies gently by, making fantastic figures as it drifts. It seems to mock paltry man-made efforts to fight it, and yet they are amazingly successful.

They depend, however, for success upon the man. Elaborate your mechanical devices as you will, the success of a lighthouse comes back to the man who keeps it. His is a dreary life, to which not many men are suited. Strange thoughts and fancies might come drifting into one's brain, as gently and slowly as the grey wisps of fog outside; and after a while some might remain, even when the fog has gone, and the water shines blue in the sunlight.

It is that way that danger lies. In the crowded waterways where inspectors are many and inspections numerous, the risk is small, for the loneliness is not so great.

But there are other lighthouses where from month's end to month's end a man will see nobody but the other fellow who lives with him. Excepting the boat with supplies, there is nothing to break the deadly monotony. Sometimes, even, there is no other fellow: the man is alone. Strange things may happen then if those drifting thoughts and fancies come and take root – there is danger ahead. The step between sanity and madness is not great, and once it has been taken there is no safe return.

Corn Reef was one of those other lighthouses.

We were drifting homewards in one of those small coasting boats which call at unknown islands and deal in strange cargoes, and it happened that one day in spring we came back to Tampico, the island which held the grave of the husband of the only woman who mattered to Jim. We took rooms in the hotel, and almost as if the words had been spoken aloud I heard again her voice saying: "Oh, you cur!"

I think Jim heard it too, for suddenly he smiled at me a little bitterly.

"Is it much use going home, Dick?" he said. He didn't wait for my answer, but turned away while I strolled down to the club. Nothing had changed; nothing ever will change at Tampico. The club looked just as I left it, two years before.

It was unoccupied save for one man, who glanced up as I came in, and then went on reading the letter he held in his hand. Every now and then he gave a little frown. I looked at him covertly. There was that nameless something about him which marked him instantly as one of those thousands of Britishers who spend their lives in little-known quarters of the globe, carrying on the jobs of Empire. They generally die of disease, unknown and unthanked, or return to England in the fullness of time and sink into obscurity in a London suburb. But while they're in harness they live, and when the harness drops off they don't mind dying. So perhaps it doesn't matter very much.

With a three-months-old illustrated paper in my hand, I sat down and forgot about him. He did not seem disposed for conversation, nor was I. I was feeling lazy; and it wasn't until I heard Jim behind me cheerfully greeting the stranger that I realised I was holding the paper upside down.

"Why, it's MacGregor," I heard him say. "The last time I saw you was in Singapore. How are you, my dear fellow?"

"Jim Maitland, by all that's wonderful!"

The stranger got up and seized Jim's hand, and just then Jim caught sight of me.

"Come over here, Dick," he cried. "This is Jock MacGregor, and a mad Government pays him a salary to cruise outlandish waters and see that no one has walked off with a lighthouse or two."

"Salary!" snorted MacGregor. "Call my beggarly pittance a salary! And now the blighters have put a survey job on to my shoulders as well. They think I haven't enough work to do, I suppose."

"But what brings you here, Jock?" asked Jim. "Tampico is a bit out of your beaten track, isn't it?"

MacGregor nodded and the frown reappeared.

"The supply-boat for the lighthouse at Corn Reef goes from here," he said. "It starts tomorrow, and I'm going with it."

"Visit of inspection?" said Jim.

"Yes and no," returned the other. "In all probability I shall stay there for a week or so."

Jim raised his eyebrows.

"Stay?" he said. "I thought you merely looked in to see that the keeper hadn't been frying sausages on the lamps."

MacGregor grinned, then grew serious again.

"That's why I said 'yes and no.' This isn't an ordinary inspection." He hesitated, then leant forward. "Care to hear the story, Jim?"

"Get it right off your chest, Jock," he said.

"Well, if it won't bore you, I will," began MacGregor. "Only I'll have to go back a bit. When we last met, I had nothing to do with this area at all. Bill Lambert had it, and mine was farther north. Bill took to seeing things that weren't there, and has recently gone on permanent sick leave. They said they'd send a successor, as they always do say, but so far there's been no sign of him; and until his arrival Mr MacGregor was to carry on with both areas – and no increase of pay, bless their hearts! However, I didn't mind, and in normal circumstances it would have made no odds to me. If you have twice the area to cover, you do half the number of inspections, and it comes to the same thing in the end. It's just a matter of form and routine, as you can guess – in normal circumstances."

He emphasised the last three words, and Jim glanced at him.

"One gathers that Corn Reef is not quite normal?" he remarked.

"I'm coming to that," said MacGregor. "I don't know whether you know the part or not – personally, I know it only from the map. Corn Reef sticks out from a smallish island called Taba Island, which I believe is inhabited by a few natives. It stretches about halfway across a deep-water channel towards the next of the group, which is uninhabited. Beyond that come other small islands and reefs. The only method of navigating the belt is through the other half of the deep-water channel I have told you about – one-half of which is blocked by Corn Reef.

"The lighthouse stands on the end of the reef, midway across the channel. At low water it can be reached on foot; at high water the reef is covered. So much for the locality; now for the personal details. Six months ago, as I said, I took over from Bill Lambert. It was an informal sort of taking over, as he was pretty bad, and I got no information out of him. But it didn't worry me much, as I'd no idea then that there was anything peculiar in his area. It wasn't till a month ago, when I received a communication from the keeper at Corn Reef lighthouse, that I began to look into things. His name is David Temple, and the communication was brief and to the point. It stated that his assistant, when attending to the bell, had been drowned. Could another be sent?"

"Bell?" said Jim. "I don't follow."

"Sorry," said MacGregor. "I forgot. At certain times you get a thick belt of fog across the reef and the channel, stretching right along the islands. Probably it's heavy ground mist. When that comes down they use a huge bell, which is tolled by machinery. It is built out on a sort of platform below the level of the light – it seems a pretty antiquated sort of arrangement. However, there it is, and as long as it works you won't get them to spend money on anything more up to date.

"Well, when I got Temple's letter I began looking up the files. To my amazement I found that about three months before Bill Lambert went a precisely similar letter had reached *him*. At first I thought that the second was merely a reminder, and that Bill had forgotten. So I made inquiries, only to discover the sinister fact that it was far from a reminder. Bill *had* sent a new man. Within nine months, two men at Corn Reef had been drowned. Which seemed to show that there was something radically wrong with the bell arrangements: something which I utterly failed to get at from the plans. The whole idea is antiquated, but seems perfectly safe. I could see no reason whatever, short of suicide, why two men should fall into the sea."

"And even granting that, why of necessity they should be drowned?" said Jim quietly.

MacGregor shrugged his shoulders.

"The place is alive with sharks, of course," he remarked. "But I've not quite finished yet. Another unpleasant fact appeared shortly after this letter from Temple. I ran into a skipper at Singapore, and he was after Bill Lambert's blood. When he heard I was doing Bill's job he turned his wrath on me. His accusation amounted to this: that on the morning of February 24th he was on the bridge of his ship, nosing her gently through a thick mist. Suddenly there came a bellow from the look-out man, and to his horror he saw, looming out of the mist on the starboard side – Corn Reef lighthouse.

"'I could have spat an orange pip at it, and hit it,' he said to me. 'I could almost have touched it with my hand. In thirty years I've never had such an escape. Another six inches, and we'd have been on that reef.'

"'But wasn't the bell ringing?' I demanded.

"'Not a sound!' he roared. 'Not a sound. You can hear that bell for fifteen miles – and there wasn't a sound. As I passed by, I looked up. Man! I tell you the bell was ringing right enough – I could see it through the fog – but no sound came. But above the beat of the engine I thought I heard a steady thud, thud, thud in time with the beat of the bell. But maybe it was my imagination.'"

Jock MacGregor paused.

"So that is the rather peculiar situation I'm up against," he said grimly.

"And how do you propose to deal with it?"

"Temple asked for an assistant," said MacGregor, "and he's going to have one – me." He lit a cigarette, and leaned back in his chair. "There's something wrong, Jim," he continued after a moment, "very wrong. That merchant skipper was a hard-headed customer, and if he saw that bell moving – it was moving. Then why was there no sound? And then two men drowned in nine months! I guess I'm not going to send a third till I've had a look round myself. Temple has never seen me, so there won't be any difficulty in passing myself off."

Jim was looking thoughtfully out of the window. "How long has Temple been there?" he said.

"Years, as far as I can make out," answered MacGregor. "A paper in the file, dated five years ago, showed that he had asked to stay on. There is no vast rush for Corn Reef, and I suppose Bill Lambert was only too glad to let him."

Jim shook his head.

"Five years is a long time, Jock," he said gravely, "far too long in a place like that."

"You think I may find Temple a bit queer?"

Jim shrugged his shoulders.

"Jock," he said, "I've got a proposal to make to you. Temple doesn't know me either. You go as his assistant. I'll go as your new boss. Dick can come as a pal of mine. If everything seems right, we shall all have had a pleasant trip, and Temple will be none the worse. If things are not all right – three heads are better than one, Jock."

"I accept with the greatest pleasure," said MacGregor. "To tell you the strict truth, it's a great relief."

Of the run to Taba Island I shall say nothing. The first part was uninteresting, and the last few miles so beautiful as to defy description. In front stretched the belt of islands, with the lighthouse standing up ahead. On our left lay Taba Island, a riot of tropical vegetation and glorious flowers right down to the water, broken by stretches of golden sand.

Between lighthouse and island was a line of surf marking Corn Reef; to the right of the lighthouse lay the deep-water channel of unbroken blue. As we got nearer we could see the strange structure on the deep-water side which marked the position of the bell. It reminded one of those medieval galleries jutting out from the walls of old castles, from which the defenders used to pour burning oil on the gentlemen below.

"Great Scott!" said Jim. "If that fellow passed close enough to see that bell in a fog, I don't wonder he wanted somebody's blood."

We were now near enough to see details. On a rough landing stage at the foot of the lighthouse a man was standing gazing at us through a telescope. As we came close he shut it up and awaited us with folded arms. He was dressed in white, and might have been carved out of stone, so motionless did he stand. Then he spoke in a curiously harsh voice.

"Which is my new assistant?"

He was tall and gaunt, with a coarse straggling beard, and I could conceive no worse fate than being condemned to spend month after month alone with him.

It was Jim who answered as we had arranged.

"Here is your new assistant – MacGregor. I am your new inspector in place of Mr Lambert."

"You will find everything in good order, sir," he said quietly, but staring at Jock MacGregor.

"How comes it that two men have been drowned within such a short time, Temple?" demanded Jim sternly. "There must have been gross carelessness somewhere."

"It is the bell, sir," answered the man, still in the same quiet voice. "When the mist comes down and presses round one's head it is sometimes difficult to see."

Jim grunted, and eyed the man narrowly.

"Then the bell must be removed," he said.

Temple started violently.

"It is only carelessness, sir, on their parts," he cried. "The bell has never hurt me."

"Well, I will inspect everything," said Jim curtly. "I shall stay here until the supply boat returns the day after tomorrow."

I saw Temple shoot a suspicious glance at him, but he merely nodded and said, "Very good, sir."

Then he glanced towards Taba Island and nodded as if satisfied.

"There will be fog tonight, sir," he remarked. "When the Queen of the Island is crowned in mist at this time of day there is always fog. So you will hear the bell."

He went off to superintend the disposal of his stores, and Jim turned to MacGregor.

"What on earth is he talking about, Jock?" he muttered.

"The Queen of the Island is that hill. I remember seeing it marked on the map."

"He seems a strange sort of bird."

"You're right, Jim," MacGregor said. "But he doesn't strike me as anything out of the way. You meet some queer customers on this game."

Certainly during the next hour there seemed nothing peculiar about Temple. Jim asked a few leading questions, but for the most part he let the other man talk. We examined the mirrors, reflectors, and lamps; but most of all we examined Temple himself. Then we came to the bell.

It looked enormous from close to. It was carried on a steel cantilever arm, and, about eight feet below, a narrow wooden platform, some eighteen inches wide, jutted out over the water. It was little more than a plank ten feet long, and though railings made it perfectly safe, it gave one a feeling of dizziness. Above hung the bell with its motionless clapper; below lay the water. Poised between them was the platform, all too narrow for my liking.

"Was it from here that the two men fell?"

"Yes, sir," said Temple quietly. "Though I did not see it happen myself. I was inside attending to the mechanism that works the bell."

"And did you make no effort to save them?"

Temple peered over the side for a moment or two, then pointed downwards without a word. I counted three evil shapes glide by in the clear depths.

"And when did the last man fall over?" went on Jim. "On what date?"

"On February 24th, sir," said Temple, and MacGregor caught his breath. "It was in the early morning when the fog was thick. It is entered in my log book."

"Was the bell ringing at the time?"

"The bell always rings when there is a fog, sir," answered Temple, and Jim glanced at MacGregor, who shook his head imperceptibly. "Would you care to hear it now, and see how it works?"

"Yes," said Jim, "I should."

"There is a heavy weight inside the lighthouse, sir," said Temple. "It works the bell by means of cogged wheels." He sounded like someone patiently explaining to a child. "If you will come inside, I will start it."

We followed him in, and he pressed down a lever. Almost at once the bell began to swing, slightly at first, gradually increasing until at length the first deep note rang out. The notes came deeper and more resonant, till at last both clapper and bell settled down to a rhythmic swing. Like a huge pendulum the clapper passed backwards and forwards over the platform outside, while the bell swung down to meet it, first one side, then the other. The booming note seemed to fill the whole universe with one vast volume of sound. It deadened one's brain; it stunned one; it made one gasp for breath.

Suddenly I felt Jim grip my arm. Speech was impossible, but I followed the direction of his eyes. He was looking at David Temple; so was Jock MacGregor.

The lighthouse keeper was staring at the Queen of the Island with blazing eyes. His hands were locked together, and he was muttering something, while the sweat glistened on his forehead.

He seemed to have forgotten our existence, and when Jim touched him on the shoulder he swung round with a hideous snarl.

"Stop the bell!" shouted Jim, and the snarl vanished. He was the subordinate again, though in his eyes there was a look of sly cunning.

He pressed another lever, and the bell gradually ceased, till at last it swung in silence, save for a faint creaking.

"Is that satisfactory, sir?" asked Temple quietly. "I would like to stow away my stores, and then go through my log with you."

Jim nodded. "All right, Temple."

The man went out, and we stared at one another thoughtfully.

"February 24th," said MacGregor. "Did you note that, Jim?"

"I noted it right enough," answered Jim. "Jock, the man's queer. Did you see his face while that infernal bell was ringing, and he was staring at the mountain yonder?"

MacGregor had strolled over to the window himself, and suddenly he beckoned to us.

"Come here," he muttered. "Look at him now."

Below, on the landing stage, knelt David Temple with his arms flung out towards the mist-crowned mountain. For half a minute he stayed there motionless; then he rose and came in.

"He's worse than queer," said MacGregor. "He's mad."

Now I come to what happened when the mist came down. Jim and I had spent the night in the room normally used by the assistant, while Jock MacGregor had stopped in the other room to take his turn with the lamp. At the faintest sign of trouble he was to call us, and, to make doubly sure, Jim and I had taken it in turns to stay awake. It was no good letting Temple see we suspected anything, since no steps could be taken till the return of the supply boat. Then Jock MacGregor had decided that Temple was to go back while he remained in the lighthouse till a relief was sent.

During the evening Temple had been perfectly rational, though I had caught him once or twice eyeing MacGregor with a curiously furtive expression. He had lit the light and explained the simple mechanism, and then had stood with us while we watched the beam sweep the water below. It was a glorious night, without a trace of fog, and for a time our suspicions were lulled. Only once did a remark of Temple's bring back our doubts.

"The Queen is angry tonight," he said, staring at the island. "She demands a sacrifice."

"What do you mean?" said Jim sternly.

"When she veils her head, sir," he answered quietly, "her subjects must appease her. Otherwise she will be revenged."

He left the room with a word of apology, and we heard him going downstairs.

"Native superstition," grunted MacGregor.

"Perhaps," said Jim. "But once native superstition gets a white man, Jock, look out."

That is all that had happened before we turned in: little enough to prepare us for what was to come later. It must have been about three o'clock when Jim roused me to take my turn, and we heard a ship's siren wail in the distance. We heard it a second time. For a moment it made no impression on our minds, then the same thought struck us both.

We dashed to the window and looked out into a thick mist that drifted slowly past, blotting out everything. No water could be seen, no star – just dense clammy vapour. The fog had come down on Corn Reef – and the bell was silent.

Once again the siren wailed mournfully, and then, as we listened, we heard a steady creaking and then a strange dull thudding noise – creak, thud; creak, thud!

Jim sprang to the door-handle; but the door refused to budge. We had been locked in. Jock MacGregor was alone with a madman. Even as we realised it there came a faint shout of "Help!"

It took six shots to shatter the lock. We dashed up the short flight of stairs into the room above. Confronting us was David Temple with an iron bar in his hands. His face was the face of a maniac. But it wasn't at him we were looking – it was beyond him to the place where the platform stretched into the mist. The door was open, and we could see the great bell swinging to and fro. Lashed loosely to the end of the clapper, and clinging to it desperately, was Jock MacGregor.

"The Queen demands a sacrifice," roared the madman. "Two she has had, and now she requires a third. Stand back!"

There was no time for half-measures. MacGregor's voice, breathless and gasping, came to us faintly: "For heaven's sake, hurry!" And out of the mist, much louder and nearer, wailed the siren.

Jim rushed in somehow; the crowbar crashed to the floor. Even then Temple tried to stop us, but a blow on the point of the jaw put him to sleep. Then began a desperate race against time. Outside the siren was going continuously, seeming almost on top of us. Standing on the platform we tried to catch MacGregor as he swung past us. But the bell was heavy, and it seemed an age before we could check the clapper sufficiently to cut him down. Every moment we expected to hear the ship strike rock. But at last we had him down, and Jim darted to the lever to restart the bell.

The first deep boom rang out, and in the silence before the swing became regular we heard a sudden agonised shout, and the thrashing of a propeller. Then the bell tolled again, and again. All outside sound was drowned; only the bell crashed out its message of warning.

So three sweating men sat and waited for the mist to lift off Corn Reef, while David Temple sat in a corner smiling happily to himself, nodding his head in time with the bell. He had put a drug, we discovered, in Jock MacGregor's coffee, and the next thing MacGregor knew, he found himself swinging violently through space, to stop even more violently as he hit the side of the bell. How even a madman had had the strength to lift a full-grown man and lash him to the clapper was a mystery till we discovered some rough steps of the housemaid variety, and even with them immense strength was required. But he had done it, and for ten minutes MacGregor had swung backwards and forwards, dazed and half-stunned, while the madman had crouched below him with his arms flung out towards the Queen of the Island.

At seven o'clock the mist lifted, and we stopped that accursed bell. Out to sea lay a steamer, and a boat was being lowered. Through glasses we saw an officer get in, and then the boat was pulled to the lighthouse.

I have met angry men in my life, but nothing like the speechless fury of the skipper of the good ship *Floriana*. I don't blame him, for his eyes still held the look of a badly frightened man.

We told him the story, and Temple smiled placidly in his corner. After a while the skipper apologised handsomely. He went out to look at the bell, and for a while we stood on the platform. Then the skipper leant forward, peering at the inside of the bell. In silence he pointed to two dull stains which we had not noticed. They were just where the clapper hit the bell – one on each side, and they were a rusty red.

"Two assistants, you say?" he grunted. "What a death!"

I looked down into the blue water. Three more evil shapes glided by and disappeared. Then I looked at Taba Island. Clear and beautiful in the morning sun the Queen of the Island rose to the sky. Her crown had disappeared.

CHAPTER 8

The Seven Missionaries

It never really got much beyond the rumour stage. Captain James Kelly, of the SS *Andaman*, saw to that. It wouldn't have done him or his line any good, and since England was troubled with railway strikes and war scares, doings on the other side of the globe were apt to be crowded out of the newspapers.

But he couldn't stop the rumour, and "Our Special Correspondent" in Colombo made out quite a fair story for his paper at home. It didn't appear: seemingly the editor thought the man had taken to drink. In fact, all that did appear were two short and apparently disconnected notices. The first was found under shipping intelligence:

The SS *Andaman* arrived yesterday at Colombo. She remained to carry out repairs to her wireless, and will leave tomorrow for Plymouth.

The second appeared some two or three months later:

No news has yet been heard of the SY *Firefly*, which left Colombo some months ago for an extensive cruise in the Indian Ocean. It is feared that she may have foundered with all hands in one of the recent gales.

But she didn't. The sea was dead calm when the SY *Firefly* went down in the thousand fathoms of water not far from the Cocos Islands; and but for the grace of Heaven and Jim Maitland that fate would have overtaken the *Andaman* instead.

The SS *Andaman* was a vessel of some three thousand tons – a cargo boat carrying passengers. There was only one class, and accommodation for about thirty people. Twelve knots was her maximum speed, and she quivered like a jelly if you tried to get more out of her. Last, but not least, Captain Kelly had been her skipper for ten years, and loved her profoundly.

When Jim and I went on board she was taking in cargo, and Kelly was having words with the harbour master over something; the argument had reached the dangerous stage of politeness. But Jim had sailed in her before, and a minute or two later a delighted chief steward was shaking him warmly by the hand.

"This is great, sir!" he cried. "We got a wireless about the berths, but we had no idea it was from you."

"You can fix us up, Bury?" asked Jim.

"Sure thing, Mr Maitland," answered the other. "We've only got twelve on board – two Yanks, a coloured gentleman, two ladies, and a missionary bunch."

We had followed him below, and he was showing us our cabins.

"Seven of them, sir," he went on; "with two crates of literature, all complete. Maybe you saw them sitting around on deck."

"Can't say I did, Bury," said Jim indifferently.

"They never go ashore, sir," continued the steward. "There they sit from morning till night, till they fairly give you the hump."

"It doesn't sound like one long scream of excitement," said Jim. "But if they are happy, that's all that matters. Come on, Dick, let's go up and see if old man Kelly is still being polite."

We went on deck to find that the argument was finished, and with a shout of delight the skipper recognised Jim. Jim went forward, and I stood idly watching the scene on the quay.

Then, quite distinctly, I heard a voice from behind me:

"By heaven, it's Jim Maitland!"

The remark was so ordinary, so completely expected when Jim was about, that I never gave it a thought, at least not till Jim's voice hailed me.

It was then that I noticed two benevolent-looking clergymen seated close to me in deck-chairs, their eyes on the skipper and Jim. Not another soul was in sight, and I had no doubt that it was one of them who had spoken. As I stood talking with the skipper and Jim my mind was working.

There was no reason, to be sure, why a missionary should not recognise Jim, but somehow it seemed odd. So did the tone in which it had been spoken. However, the matter was a small one, and I should probably have dismissed it from my mind, but for the sequel a minute or so later.

The skipper was called away on some matter, and Jim and I strolled back past the two parsons. They both looked up with mild interest as we passed, but neither gave the faintest sign of recognition.

That did strike me as strange: why should they utterly ignore a man whom they evidently knew?

"Come and lean over the side, Jim," I said when we were out of earshot. "There's something a little funny I want to tell you. Only don't look round."

When I had finished he shrugged his shoulders.

"More people know Tom Fool, old boy, than Tom Fool knows. I certainly don't know either of them, but it's more than likely they know me by sight."

Evidently Jim was inclined to dismiss the episode as trifling, and after a time I agreed. Even at lunch that day, when the skipper was formally introducing us and the clergymen still gave no sign, I thought no more about it.

The man whose voice I had heard turned out to be the leader of the band, the Reverend Samuel Longfellow, and his destination was Colombo. They were going to open a mission somewhere in Ceylon and run it on lines of their own. Apparently no such place existed belonging to their particular denomination. They seemed very decent fellows, even if they did not greatly add to the general gaiety.

The voyage pursued its normal course for the first four or five days. The two Americans and the skipper made up the necessary numbers for a game of poker; the two ladies – a mother and daughter named Armstrong – knitted; the seven parsons read; and the coloured gentleman effaced himself.

The weather was perfect, and the sea like a mill-pond, with every prospect of continuing so for some time. So we lazed along at our twelve knots, making a couple of final calls before starting on the two thousand mile run to Colombo.

It was the first night out on the last stage that Jim and I were sitting talking with the skipper on the bridge, where, being a privileged person, Jim was allowed. Occasionally the sharp hissing crackle of the wireless broke the silence, and we could see the operator in his shirt-sleeves through the open door of his cabin.

"I guess it's hard to begin to estimate what we sailor men owe to Marconi for that invention," said Kelly thoughtfully. "It seems almost incredible how we got along without it. And what can I do for you, sir?"

An abrupt change in his tone made me look round to see the Reverend Samuel standing behind us. He evidently felt he was trespassing, for his voice was almost apologetic.

"Is it possible, Captain," he asked, "to send a message by your wireless?"

"Of course," answered Kelly. "Hand any message to the operator, and he'll send it for you."

"You see, I've never sent by wireless before," said the parson mildly, "and I wasn't quite sure what to do. Can you get an answer quickly?"

"That depends on whom you are sending it to, and where he is."

"He's on a yacht somewhere near," answered the clergyman. "He is a missionary like myself, whose health has broken down, and a kind friend is taking him for a cruise to help him recover. I felt it would be so nice if I could speak to him, so to say, and hear how he is getting on."

"Quite," agreed the skipper gravely. "Well, Mr Longfellow, there is nothing to prevent your speaking to him as much as you like. The operator will send down the answer as soon as he receives it."

"Oh, thank you, Captain Kelly," said the parson gratefully. "I suppose there's no way of saying where I am?" he continued hesitatingly. "I mean, when one sends an ordinary wire the receiver can look up where you are on the map, and it makes it so much more interesting for him."

The skipper knocked out his pipe.

"I'm afraid, Mr Longfellow," he remarked at length in a stifled voice, "that you can't quite do that at sea. Of course, the latitude and longitude of the ship will be given on the message, so the navigating officer of his yacht will be able to show your friend with a pin exactly where you were in the Indian Ocean when the message was sent."

"I see," said the clergyman. "How interesting! And then, if I tell him that we are moving straight towards Colombo at twelve knots an hour, my dear friend will be able to follow me in spirit all the way on the map?"

The skipper choked slightly.

"Precisely, Mr Longfellow. But I wouldn't call it twelve knots *an hour*. Just twelve knots."

"Twelve knots. I see. Thank you so much. I don't know much about the sea. May I go now to the gentleman who sends the messages?"

"By all means," said Kelly, and Jim's shoulders shook. "Give the operator your message, and you shall have the answer when it arrives."

Again murmuring his thanks, the missionary departed, and we saw him in earnest converse with the operator. That worthy, having read the message and scratched his head, stared a little dazedly at the Reverend Samuel Longfellow, obviously doubting his sanity. To be asked to dispatch to the world at large a message beginning "Dear brother," and finishing "Yours in the Church," struck him as being one of those things which a self-respecting wireless operator does not do.

"Poor bird!" said the skipper thoughtfully. "I'm glad he doesn't know what the bulk of our cargo is this trip. He wouldn't be able to sleep at nights for fear of pirates."

Jim looked up lazily.

"Why, what have you got on board, old man?"

The skipper lowered his voice.

"I haven't shouted about it, Jim, and I don't think the crew know. Don't pass it on – but we have over half a million in gold below, to say nothing of pearls worth another quarter."

Jim whistled. "By Jove! it would be a nice haul for someone. A bit out of your line, isn't it, James, carrying specie?"

"It is," the other agreed. "It generally goes on the bigger boats, but there was some hitch. It's just as safe with me as with them. Wireless has killed piracy. Still, it's a big feather in my cap getting away with this consignment. It's going to make the trip worth six ordinary ones to the firm, and to me. With any luck I have hopes that it will no longer be out of our line. We might get a share of that traffic, and I'll be able to buy that chicken farm in Dorsetshire earlier than I thought."

Jim laughed. "You old humbug, James! You'll never give up the sea."

The skipper sighed and stretched himself.

"Maybe not, lad – till she gives me up, anyway. But chickens are nice birds, they tell me, and Dorset is England."

A few minutes later a sudden explosion of mirth came from the wireless operator.

"What is it, Jenkins?" called the skipper.

"Message for the parson, sir," answered the operator. "There is a duplicate on the table."

He saluted, and went after the Reverend Samuel.

"I think," murmured the skipper, with a twinkle, "that I will now inspect the wireless installation. Would you care to come with me?"

This is what we read:

DEAR BROTHER how lovely the gentleman who guides our ship tells me we pass quite close about midday the day after tomorrow will wave pocket-handkerchief. FERDINAND.

"My sainted aunt!" spluttered the skipper. "Wave a pocket-handkerchief!"

"I think I prefer 'the gentleman who guides our ship,'" said Jim gravely. "Anyway, James, I shall borrow your telescope as we come abreast of Ferdinand. I'd just hate to miss him. Good night, old man. You must have that message framed."

About half an hour later the door of my cabin opened and Jim entered abruptly. I was lying smoking a final cigarette, and I looked at him in surprise. He was fully dressed, though I had seen him begin taking off his clothes twenty minutes before, and he was looking grave.

"Pay attention, Dick," he said quietly. "I'd just got my coat off when I remembered I'd left my cigar-case on deck. I went up to get it – and I heard my own name mentioned. Naturally I listened, and I distinctly heard this: 'Don't forget – you are absolutely responsible for Maitland.' I couldn't catch anything else except a few disconnected words here and there, such as 'wireless,' 'midday.' Then there was a general pushing-back of deck-chairs, and the black-coated seven trooped off to bed. They didn't see me; they were on the other side of the funnel – but it made me think. Well, why the deuce is this bunch of parsons so interested in me? I don't like it, Dick." He looked at me hard through his eyeglass. "Do you think they really are parsons?"

I sat up in bed with a jerk.

"What do you mean? Of course they're parsons. Why shouldn't they be parsons?"

Jim thoughtfully lit a cigar.

"Quite – why shouldn't they be? At the same time – " He paused, and blew out a cloud of smoke. "Dick, I suppose I'm a suspicious bird, but this peculiar interest in me is strange, to say the least of it. Let us suppose they are not parsons. Well, I have a fairly well-known reputation as a tough customer if trouble occurs."

"Just exactly what do you mean, Jim?" I demanded.

He answered my question by another.

"Don't you think that that wireless answer was a bit *too* foolish to be genuine?"

"But Jenkins took it down in front of our eyes."

"Oh, it was sent – I'm not denying that – just as he received it and we read it. But was it sent by a genuine parson, cruising in a genuine yacht for his health? If so, my opinion of the brains of the Church drops below par. But if it was sent by someone who wished to pose as the silly curate of fiction – "

"Look here," I said. "I may be several sorts of ass, but I can't get you. Why should anyone not only pose as a parson, but also send fool messages round the universe?"

"Has it occurred to you," said Jim quietly, "that those two fool messages included two very useful pieces of information? First, our exact position at a given moment, our course and speed. Secondly, the approximate time when the sick curate's friend's yacht will impinge on that course. A third fact, not contained in either message, but possibly with a bearing on things, is that half million in gold and that quarter of a million in pearls."

"Good heavens!" I muttered.

"Mark you, Dick, I may have stumbled into a real first-class mare's nest. But I don't like the Reverend Samuel's tender solicitude for my safety."

"Are you going to say anything to the skipper?"

"Yes. But he's a pig-headed fellow, and he'll probably be darned rude. I should, if I were in his shoes. They aren't worrying over *his* salvation."

With that he went to bed, leaving me thinking hard. Could there be anything in it? Could anyone really attempt piracy in the twentieth century? It was ridiculous, and the next morning I went round to tell Jim so. His cabin was empty, and there was a note lying on the bed addressed to me. It was brief and to the point.

I am ill in bed with a sharp dose of fever. Pass the good news on. – JIM.

I did say so at breakfast, and I thought I detected a shade of relief pass over the face of the Reverend Samuel, though he inquired about the sufferer, and even wished to give him some remedy of his own. But I assured him that quinine and quiet were all that were required, coupled with a starvation diet, and with that the matter dropped.

Then there began a time of irritating suspense. Not a sign of Jim did I see for the whole of that day and the following night. His door had been locked since before breakfast, and I didn't even know if he was inside or not. But I did know that something was doing, and few things are more annoying than being out of a game you know is being played. Afterwards I realised that it was unavoidable, but at the time I was annoyed.

The strange thing is that when the thing did occur it came with almost as much of a shock to me as if I had had no suspicions. It was the suddenness of it, and the absolute absence of any fuss or shouting. Naturally, I didn't see the whole thing: my outlook was limited to what actually happened to me and near by.

It was about half-past eleven, and I was strolling on deck. Midday had been the time mentioned, and I was feeling excited and restless. Mrs Armstrong and her daughter were seated in their usual place, and I stopped and spoke to them. Usually Mrs Armstrong was the talker of the two – a big gaunt woman with yellow spectacles, but pleasant and homely. This morning, however, the daughter answered, and her mother, who wore a veil in addition to her spectacles, sat silently beside her.

"Poor mother has such a headache from the glare," she said. "I hope Mr Maitland is better."

I murmured something just as two of the parsons strolled past, and I wondered why the girl gave a little laugh. Then suddenly she sat up.

"Oh! look at that lovely yacht!"

I swung round quickly, and there, sure enough, about a hundred yards from us, and just coming into sight round the awning, was a small steam yacht. And at that moment the shorter of the parsons put a revolver within an inch of my face, while the other ran his hands over my pockets. It was so unexpected that I gaped at him foolishly; and even when I saw my revolver flung overboard I hardly realised that the big hold-up had begun.

There came a heavy thud from just above us, and I saw Jenkins, the wireless man, pitched forward on his face half out of his cabin door. He lay there while another of the parsons wrecked his instruments with the iron bar he had used to stun the operator. With a squawk of terror like a startled hen, Mrs Armstrong rose, with her pink parasol in one hand and her rug in the other, and fled towards the bows. She looked so funny that I couldn't help it – I laughed. Even the two parsons smiled, though not for long.

"Go below," said one of them to Miss Armstrong. "Remain in your cabin. And you" – he turned to me – "go aft where the others are."

"You scoundrel!" I shouted, "what are you playing at?"

"Don't argue, or I'll blow out your brains," he said quietly. "And get a move on."

I found the two Americans and the coloured gentleman in a bunch with a few deck hands. Everyone seemed dazed. One of the so-called parsons stood near with a revolver in each hand, but it was really unnecessary: we were none of us in a position to do anything.

Suddenly one of the Americans gripped my arm.

"Gee! look at the two guns on that yacht."

Sure enough, mounted fore and aft, and trained directly on us, were two guns of about three-inch calibre; and behind each stood two men.

"What's the game, anyway?" he went on excitedly, as two boats shot away from the yacht.

For the first time I noticed that the engines had stopped, and that we were lying motionless on the calm oily sea. But my principal thoughts were with Jim. Where was he? What was he doing? Had these blackguards done away with him, or was he hiding? Even so, what could he do? Those two guns had an unpleasant appearance.

A bunch of armed men poured over the side and disappeared below, only to come up again carrying a number of wooden boxes, which they lowered into the boats alongside. They worked with the efficiency of well-trained sailors, and I found myself shouting aloud. For I knew what was inside those boxes, and was utterly helpless to do anything. Yet I couldn't help a sort of unwilling admiration: the thing was so perfectly organised. It might have been a well-rehearsed drill instead of a gigantic piece of piracy.

I stepped back a few paces, and looked up at the bridge. The skipper was there with his three officers, covered by another parson. The fifth member of the party was the Reverend Samuel Longfellow. He was smiling gently to himself, and as the last of the boxes was lowered he came to the edge of the bridge and addressed us.

"We are now going to leave you," he remarked. "You are all unarmed, and I wish to give you a word of advice. Should either of the gunners on my yacht see anyone move before we are on board, he will open fire. So, Captain Kelly, do not be tempted to have a shot at me, because it will be the last shot you ever have. You will now join your crew, if you please."

In silence the skipper and his officers came down, and the speaker followed. For a moment he stood facing us with an ironical smile on his face.

"Your brother in the Church," he remarked, "thanks you for your little gift to his collection." Then, "Is it set?" he asked briefly.

"Yes," said the other. "We'd better hurry. What about that woman up there?"

"Confound her!" answered the Reverend Samuel. "A pleasant journey, Captain Kelly."

He stepped down the gangway into the second boat, and was pulled away towards the yacht.

Then for the first time I remembered Mrs Armstrong. She was cowering down with her hands over her ears, the picture of abject terror. But now curiosity overcame her fright and she knelt up and stared at the yacht. Her pink parasol was clutched in her hands, and tragic though the situation was, I could not help smiling.

A mocking shout from the yacht made me look away again. The scoundrel who called himself the Reverend Samuel Longfellow was standing beside the boxes of gold and pearls stacked on the deck. He was bowing ironically, with the six other blackguards beside him, when the last amazing development took place.

Literally before our eyes they vanished in a great sheet of flame. I had a momentary glimpse of the yacht apparently splitting in two, and then the roar of a gigantic explosion nearly deafened me.

"Get under cover!" yelled the skipper, and there was a general stampede as bits of metal and wood began falling into the sea all round us. Then there came another smaller explosion as the sea rushed into the yacht's engine-room. A great column of water shot up, and when it subsided the yacht had disappeared.

"What in Heaven's name happened?" said one of the Americans dazedly.

I felt too dazed to reply. I looked towards the bows. Mrs Armstrong had disappeared.

The skipper sent away a boat, but it was useless. There was a mass of floating wreckage, but no trace of any survivor.

I met Mrs Armstrong half an hour later.

"Dreadful! Terrible!" she cried. "How more than thankful I am I didn't see it!"

I stared at her.

"You didn't see it?" I said. "But surely – "

And then I heard Jim's voice behind me.

"Mrs Armstrong, I have a dreadful confession to make. Mrs Armstrong, Dick, was good enough to lend me some clothes this morning, so that we could have some sport when crossing the Line – and I've gone and dropped her parasol overboard."

"We're nowhere near the Line," I remarked, but fortunately the good lady paid no attention.

"What does it matter?" she cried. "To think of that in face of this awful tragedy!"

She walked away like an agitated hen, and Jim smiled grimly.

"Poor old soul!" he said. "Let's hope she never gets an idea of the truth."

"So it was you up in the bows," I remarked.

He nodded. "Didn't you guess, Dick?"

"I went and saw Kelly that night," he went on. "At first he laughed. Then he didn't laugh so much, and presently I made a suggestion. If these men were what they said they were, the two big crates below would prove it. Let us examine them and see. Finally we went below. There were the two cases. We opened one. It was packed – not with Bibles – but with nitro-glycerine."

Jim paused.

"I don't think I have ever seen a man in such a rage as Kelly. There was a clockwork mechanism which could be started by turning a screw on the outside of each box. The whole devilish plan was as clear as daylight. There was enough stuff there to sink a fleet, and when they had cleared off with the gold we should suddenly have split in two and gone down with every soul on board."

He smiled grimly.

"I had no small difficulty in preventing James putting the whole bunch in irons on the spot, but finally I got him to agree to a plan of mine. We changed the cargo round – he and I. Their chests containing the nitro-glycerine we filled with gold, and the specie boxes we filled with nitro-glycerine and some lead and iron as a make-weight. And then we let the plan proceed. We banked on the fact that they wouldn't fool around with an hysterical old woman or a man in the throes of fever. Good girl, Miss Armstrong; she kept her mother below all the morning. And that, I think, is all."

"I'm hanged if it is!" I cried. "What made that stuff blow up, if it had been taken out of the prepared boxes?"

Jim drained his glass.

"Well," he said, "the Reverend Samuel may have dropped his cigar, or maybe something hit one of those boxes – perhaps a bullet from a gun fired near by. Come to my cabin."

I followed, and he shut the door. On the bed was Mrs Armstrong's parasol. Through a hole in the silk near the ferrule stuck the muzzle of an Express rifle. Jim took it out; then he looked at the parasol.

"Beyond repair," he said. "And since I told Mrs Armstrong I'd dropped it overboard, well – "

He rolled it up loosely, and threw it far out through the port-hole.

CHAPTER 9

The Pool of the Sacred Crocodile

There is no need for me to tell here how I met She who must be Obeyed. The rest of these chronicles are concerned with her, and that other She who completed Jim's half-section.

By rights, I suppose, our lives should have at once developed a certain tranquillity. But things don't always happen according to order. Certain it is that the narrowest shave of all occurred through my She. For a brief space the curtain was lifted on dark things that it is better to forget.

To most men Black Magic is a cause for contemptuous laughter. But most people feel some faint stirring of imagination at the vast dead monument of Stonehenge, see in the mind's eye that ancient temple peopled with vast crowds of fierce savages waiting in silence for the first rays of the rising sun to touch the altar, and then the wild-eyed priests; the human sacrifice to strange gods...

Thus it was in England two thousand years ago; thus it is today in many far places, where men still practise strange rites in secret places.

It is not good for a white man to dabble in those ceremonies, as Professor John Gainsford found – Gainsford the celebrated Egyptologist.

Most people by now have forgotten his name, though at the time the case aroused great interest. It may be remembered that, as the result of information given to them, the authorities raided a certain house on the right bank of the Nile about halfway between Cairo and Luxor. They found it deserted, but with one very strange feature. In the centre of the house was a large pool, almost the size of a small swimming-bath. It was filled with stagnant water. And when they drained the water away they made a very sinister discovery – a pair of spectacles. They were identified as belonging to Professor Gainsford. No other trace of him was ever found.

We let it rest at that – for we *knew*. We talked it over, Jim and Molly Tremayne, the professor's niece, and made our decision. Molly insists that it was just a sudden madness; Jim maintains that Professor John Gainsford attempted, and failed in, a cold-blooded crime, and died himself, justly.

Be that as it may, I will put down the truth of what happened on that ghastly night. For Molly Tremayne was my She who was Obeyed then, and is now.

Professor Gainsford was the last man whom one would have considered capable of evil, with his mutton-chop whiskers, his mild blue eyes blinking behind his spectacles, his coat-tails flapping behind him, and a silk pocket-handkerchief hanging out of his pocket.

It was one night at dinner that the Professor first mentioned the subject. He had omitted to put on his tie, and Molly had driven him upstairs to remedy the defect. We started to pull his leg about it. As a rule he used to take our chaffing in the mildest way; but that night he seemed strangely preoccupied. He kept shooting little bird-like glances at Molly, and was so unlike himself that we looked at one another in surprise.

Towards the end of the meal we found out the reason.

"I have had," he remarked suddenly, "an almost unbelievable stroke of luck this afternoon."

"Discovered a new beetle, Uncle John?" asked Molly with a smile.

"I have discovered," he answered solemnly, "that a secret cult thought to have become extinct centuries ago is still in existence. If so, I shall have made a discovery of staggering magnitude."

"But how did you find out about it, Uncle?" said Molly.

"By sheer accident," he remarked. "I was in the bazaar this afternoon, when there strode into the shop a native who was evidently not a Cairene. I happened to glance up, and I saw him make a sign to Yussuf which instantly made me forget everything else. It was the secret sign of this almost forgotten cult.

"A glance at Yussuf confirmed my opinion. He was positively cringing, and my excitement became intense, though outwardly I remained perfectly calm."

I caught Molly's eye, and smothered a smile.

"And what did you do then?" she asked.

"I followed him. Of course, he might refuse to say anything, and at first he did; but gradually, as he realised that I knew as much if not more than he did, he grew more communicative."

The Professor was shaking with excitement.

"There seems not the slightest doubt," he continued, "that there has been no break in the priesthood for over three thousand years. It is – What is it? What are you looking at?"

I swung round quickly. Molly was staring into the darkness beyond the tables with frightened eyes.

"A man," she said, "a horrible-looking native, was glaring at me with the most dreadful look in his eyes. He's gone now, but he looked awful."

"I'll go and see," I cried, getting up, but the Professor waved me back.

"Sit down," he said irritably. "The man hasn't done anything."

But it seemed to me that there was a nervous apprehension in the glance he threw at his niece.

"I'm sorry to be so stupid," she said. "Go on, Uncle John; tell us about your cult."

A little later we rose and went into the lounge. There was a small dance in the hotel, and when the Professor had retired, Molly and I took the floor.

"I can't tell you what that man's face was like, Dick," she said. "His eyes seemed to be dragging me towards him."

However, I soothed her fears, and after a while she forgot him. So did I, and it was not until much later that I remembered him again.

I had gone to bed, when suddenly there came an agitated knocking on my door, and I heard her voice: "Dick! Dick!"

In an instant I had opened it, to find Molly outside, trembling all over.

"What is it?" I cried.

"That man – that awful native," she gasped. "He's in the hotel. Oh Dick! – I'm terrified. I'd just got into bed, when something made me go to the door. I simply had to; I felt as if my legs weren't my own. I opened it, and there was the man. I can't tell you the look in his eyes." She shuddered violently. "Then all of a sudden he seemed to vanish."

"Vanish?" I said. "You've had a nightmare."

"But it wasn't a nightmare," she cried. "I tell you he was standing there in the passage."

I had to be firm. Very gently I insisted that she must either go back to her room, or spend the night with some woman friend in the hotel.

As luck would have it, the room of a little widow who was a pal of hers was opposite mine, and she had no objection to Molly sleeping with her.

I mentioned the matter to the Professor next morning, and, somewhat to my surprise, he took it quite seriously, shaking his head when I said I thought it was merely a dream.

"Possibly, Leyton," he remarked, "possibly not. Molly seems to have been very upset. I think a change will do her good. What do you say to us all three going to investigate? This cult – let us all start today and go to the secret place where it still flourishes."

"Have you any idea where it is?" I asked.

"Between here and Luxor," he answered. "We will take a *dahabeah*, and the exact place will be shown by the man I met in the bazaar."

"Do you think," I said, "that the priests will let you see anything?"

"Once we get to the Pool of the Sacred Crocodile," he answered, and his blue eyes were uncannily bright, "we shall have no difficulty. But Molly must come – you must see to that."

"I expect your niece would like the trip," I answered. "Anyway, here she is now."

It was while he was outlining the plan to Molly that I saw Jim Maitland.

"Hullo! Dick," came his cheerful voice. "I heard you were stopping here. How goes it?"

I murmured an excuse and followed him to a table a little distance away.

"We're going off today," I told him presently, "if we can fix up a *dahabeah* – with the old bird. He's her uncle, and he's sane on all points except Egyptology. Come and be introduced."

"I think it sounds a lovely trip, don't you, Mr Maitland?" Molly said. "My uncle wants to find some place with a most romantic name. It's called the Pool of the Sacred Crocodile."

Jim stared at her for a moment or two in silence; then, with a slight frown, he turned to the Professor.

"What on earth do you want to go there for, sir?" he asked quietly.

"Do you know it, Mr Maitland?" cried the Professor eagerly.

"I know of it," said Jim, "as the headquarters of one of the most secret and abominable cults handed down from ancient

Egypt. And I can assure you, Professor, that you will be wasting your time." I frowned at him, but Jim seemed very serious, and paid no attention.

"No white man would ever be allowed inside their temple," he said.

The Professor was blinking so fast that his glasses nearly fell off.

"I think I shall be able to arrange it, Mr Maitland," he said. "You see, I know one or two points concerning the ancient history of the cult of which even one of their leading adepts seemed in ignorance. In return for what I can give them, I am to have a copy of the ritual which has been handed down for three thousand years."

"Well," said Jim grimly, "if the rumours I have heard are true, you had better burn it unread."

But the Professor seemed not to hear. His little blinking eyes were fixed on Molly, and he was smiling gently to himself. For a while the conversation became general, and it wasn't until later that I was able to ask Jim what he had meant.

"Dick," he answered quietly, "you know that there aren't many things I'm frightened of. But this Pool of the Sacred Crocodile! – there are stories of unbelievable things which the natives whisper to one another; stories of black magic which make one pinch oneself to see if one's awake; stories of human sacrifice carried out with the most appalling rites."

I stared at him in amazement.

"But do you believe them?" I cried.

He didn't answer; he was looking over my shoulder.

"Something has happened to Miss Tremayne," he said quietly. The next instant Molly was beside me.

"Dick!" she whispered. "That native was standing outside the door of my room again as I was packing – just the same as last night."

"I'll go and find the scoundrel," I cried, and dashed upstairs. But the passage was empty.

I was just going down again, when the door of the Professor's room opened and he peered out.

"Hullo!" I said. "I thought you were out making arrangements for a *dahabeah*."

"I have made them," he answered curtly. "We start this afternoon."

He shut the door abruptly, and I went down feeling very thoughtful. For over the Professor's head, reflected in a mirror, I had seen a native. For a moment our eyes had met, then he had vanished.

Just before we left, Jim took me on one side.

"Whatever you do, Dick," he said gravely, "don't let Miss Tremayne out of either your sight or her uncle's once you get to your destination. One of you must always be with her."

"What on earth are you frightened of, Jim?" I demanded.

"I don't know, old man," he answered. "That's the trouble."

The boat was comfortable, and for two days we went slowly towards Luxor, tying up at night. We hardly saw the Professor except at meals, and then he barely spoke, but sat shooting glances at Molly until she got quite annoyed with him.

"I feel as if you were a canary," she cried, "and I was a bit of bird-seed."

There was no disguising the fact that the Professor was in a very queer mood. Towards the evening of the second day he appeared on deck with a pair of field-glasses. His hands were trembling as he searched the left bank of the river.

"We are there," he shouted.

He gave a frenzied order to the Captain, who swung his helm over and steered towards a small landing stage. Behind it the outlines of a house could be seen partially screened by a small orange grove, and on the landing stage itself there stood a native, motionless as if carved out of bronze.

We must have been still a hundred yards away when we heard a frantic commotion amongst the crew. They were jabbering wildly, and seemed to be in the utmost terror. In fact, we bumped that landing stage badly, as the men, huddled together forward, refused to use a boat-hook or make her fast. It was left to the Captain and me to tie her up, and it struck me that the Captain himself had no liking for his berthing place.

His eyes continually came round to the tall native, who had stepped on board and was talking earnestly with the Professor.

"Dick," Molly whispered, "I'm frightened. Don't leave me. That man has been looking at me just like that other. I wish we'd never come."

Suddenly the Professor came over to me.

"We are in luck," he said. "We are to be allowed to see the sacred crocodile at once."

Molly drew back.

"I don't think I want to, Uncle John," she said. "You go – and I'll stop here with Dick."

"Don't be ridiculous, child," he snapped. "You will see a sight that no white woman has seen for a thousand years: the inner temple of one of the sister cults of Ammon Ra. Come at once."

After a moment's hesitation Molly followed him. "We'd better humour him, Dick," she whispered.

The native led the way towards the house in the trees, with the Professor just behind him, and Molly and I behind. I could feel that she was trembling.

Our guide stalked slowly on towards the house. He knocked three times on the door and it swung open slowly, of its own accord. In front lay a long stone passage, lit with innumerable lamps and hung with tapestries which even I knew were priceless.

Braziers sent forth choking clouds of incense, but still there was another smell which I couldn't place at first: then I realised that it was the odour of musk.

Our guide stalked slowly on, while the Professor darted from side to side staring at the hangings on the walls. Another door opened slowly, and Molly and I stopped with a gasp of disgust, for the smell of musk had become overpowering. Once again the guide stood aside to let us pass through. It was the actual pool itself that lay in front.

It was hewn out of a sort of sandstone rock. A gallery some two yards wide stretched right round the walls at the same level as we were standing; while directly opposite us a heavy curtain concealed what appeared to be another door.

In each corner a motionless priest sat cross-legged in front of a burning brazier; and swinging from the centre of the roof was a marvellous old lamp which provided the only light. Cut into the walls were various Egyptian designs which roused the Professor to the verge of frenzy in his excitement. Finally, just in front of us there stuck out over the pool a thing that looked like a diving board. It shone yellow in the light, and with a sort of dull amazement I realised that it was solid gold.

"The actual platform of death," whispered the Professor in my ear. "Thousands of victims have stepped off that into the pool. And to think that we are the first white people to see it!"

"Good heavens!" I muttered. "Human sacrifice!"

The next instant I heard Molly give a shuddering gasp beside me.

"Look, Dick, look! Over there in the corner." Just rising above the surface was what looked like a baulk of wood. Suddenly, clear and distinct, a bell chimed out. As if in answer to a signal there was a swirl in the black oily liquid of the pool, a vast head and snout showed for a moment above the surface, and I had a glimpse of the most enormous crocodile I have ever seen.

With an effort I took my eyes away from the pool and looked up. The curtain opposite had been pulled aside, and a man was standing there staring at Molly. He was clad in some gorgeous garment, but I was looking at his sinister face. As I looked I heard Molly's voice as if from a distance:

"Take me away, Dick, take me away! That is the native again – *the* native."

It was also the native whom I had seen in the mirror in Professor John Gainsford's room.

He disappeared as suddenly as he had come, and Molly gave a sigh of relief.

"Let's get out, Dick," she said urgently, and I was only too glad to agree. Not until we smelled the scent of the orange trees around us did we breathe freely again.

"Dick – what an awful house!" said Molly.

"It was pretty fierce," I agreed. "By the way, where is the Professor?"

Molly laughed.

"It would take more than a bad smell to get him away. But nothing would induce me to go inside again – nothing. Did you see that man, Dick – the one on the other side of the pool?"

"I saw him," I answered briefly.

"What was he doing in Cairo? And why is he here, dressed like that?" She gave a little shudder, and stared across the Nile. "Dick, you may think it fanciful of me and silly, but inside that house just now I felt as if I were in the presence of something incredibly evil – and I felt it a thousand times more as that man stood there."

I nodded gravely.

"Personally, I couldn't get beyond the smell, but some pretty dreadful things have happened in that house. You saw that gold inlaid board in front of you stretching out over the pool? Well, from that, according to your uncle, human victims have been sacrificed to the crocodile."

"Dick – it can't be true!"

"I believe it is," I said. "But don't worry about it any more. Let's go on board and get something to wash this filthy taste out of our mouths."

As we stepped on to the *dahabeah* it seemed strangely quiet and deserted, but it was only after I had pressed the bell in the little dining-room three times that I began to feel uneasy. I went into the pantry and kitchen, and there was no sign of either cook or steward. I went on deck again to find the Captain. His cabin was empty, and in the crew's quarters there was not a soul to be seen. They had deserted, lock, stock and barrel.

A step on the deck made me look round, and Molly came towards me with a letter.

"It was on the sideboard, Dick," she said. "Addressed to you."

I glanced at it; to my amazement the handwriting was Jim's. And the note inside was laconic and to the point: "Get out of this at once. Don't spend the night here on any account."

I handed it to Molly without comment.

"When Jim tells you to do something," I said, "there is generally a pretty good reason for doing it. Unfortunately the whole crew – including the precious Captain – have chosen this moment to depart."

Molly heard the news calmly.

"I wonder where Mr Maitland is," she said. "He must be somewhere about to have left that note. What are we going to do, Dick?"

"Yes – what? Your uncle will never…"

The same startling thought occurred to both of us simultaneously.

"I'll go and look for him," I said, with a great deal more assurance than I really felt. "He's probably forgotten that we even exist."

"Then I'm coming too," she said quietly, and nothing I could say would dissuade her.

But this time our fears proved groundless. The Professor was coming towards us. He was muttering, and under his arm he carried a large book.

"We thought you were lost, Professor," I said.

He peered at us vaguely, then went past us, and we saw him go below.

"You were right, Dick," said Molly. "We simply don't exist at the moment."

"I'm afraid we've got to," I said gravely. "I'm going to have it out with him."

I went below to his cabin and knocked on the door.

"Professor," I cried, "I must have a talk with you. A very serious thing has happened."

I heard him muttering to himself, and after a while the door opened and he peered out.

"Go away," he said irritably. "I'm busy."

"Then it's got to wait," I said sternly. "You've got the rest of your life to study that book; but how long that will be, unless you listen to me, I can't say."

I meant to frighten him, and apparently I succeeded, for he opened the door wider.

"What do you mean?" he said nervously.

"Well, in the first place, the whole of the crew and the Captain have deserted."

"Oh, I know – I know," he cried peevishly. "They'll all come back tomorrow."

"You know?" I said, staring at him.

He blinked at me, and then looked away.

"One of the priests told me," he said at length.

In an instant all my worst fears came back.

"Look here, Professor," I said quietly, "you've got to remember that we have on board your niece, and my future wife. I believe that the gravest danger threatens us tonight. I believe that this desertion is part of a deep-laid scheme of the priests to keep us here tonight. I suggest, therefore, that we should cast off and drift. We shall go aground sooner or later; but at any rate we shan't be sitting at these people's front door."

"Quite impossible, Leyton," he cried angrily. "I'm amazed that you should even suggest it. The most ancient ritual is being given tonight for my special benefit. Do you suppose" – and he lashed himself into almost a fury – "that I shall miss it? What danger are you frightened of? You talk like a hysterical girl."

Jim's words spoken in Cairo came back to me: "I don't know, old man. That's the trouble." Confronted by the excited little man, I felt a fool. I hadn't one thing to go on, except the crew's desertion and Jim's note. To both the Professor turned a deaf ear.

"Ridiculous!" he snorted. Then suddenly his manner changed, and he smiled. "Believe me, my dear fellow – you exaggerate tremendously. Do you think for one moment that I would allow my dear niece to run into any danger? There is no suggestion that she should come tonight – or you. You can stay with her and guard her against any possible harm. That ought to be a not unpleasant task, my boy," he chuckled. "Now, off you go, and let me study this book of ritual. Time is all too short as it is."

With that I had to be content. I heard him lock his door, and then I joined Molly on deck. Night had come, and the faint scent of the orange trees filled the air. When I had told her what her uncle had said, "Don't let's worry, Dick," she whispered. "Let him go to his old crocodile, while we sit and watch the sun rise over the desert."

Now I come to what happened that night at the Pool of the Sacred Crocodile.

It was just as Molly and I were beginning to think about dinner, and had decided to go and forage for ourselves, that Abdullah, the steward, suddenly appeared and announced that it was ready.

"Where have you been?" I cried angrily. "I searched the place for you an hour ago."

He was profuse in explanations, and, though I was far from satisfied, there was nothing to be done. Dinner was ready and we sat down to it. The Professor, it appeared, had given strict orders not to be disturbed, and so we waited no longer. It was a good dinner, especially the Turkish coffee. Even Molly remarked on it as Abdullah refilled her cup...

Of course it was in my coffee – the particular drug they used, and not in Molly's. As long as I live I shall never forget my agony when I realised what was happening to me. I stood for a second or two clutching the table and trying to speak; then I crashed back.

I heard her voice from a great distance, and I tried again to speak. But it was useless; I could only see her like a badly focused photograph. Then suddenly she shrank back against the side of the saloon. She was no longer looking at me but out into the darkness.

"Uncle John!" she screamed. "Save me!..."

Hazily I realised what was coming. And I was right – only there were three of them this time. They stood on the other side of the table – the man who had been in Cairo in the centre, the man who had met us on the landing-stage on his right, and one I had not seen on his left. All were dressed in gorgeous robes like the leader's we had seen, and they stood motionless, staring at Molly.

They were hypnotising her in front of my eyes. Poor child, it didn't take long; and I saw her walking towards them round the table with short jerky steps.

As she advanced they backed step by step out of the range of vision. She, too, vanished. I heard her footsteps on the deck – then silence. Somehow I gave one desperate shout: "Jim – save her! Save Molly!"

That was my last coherent thought: a prayer to the man who had never failed me yet. Then I slept.

The lamp was guttering out when I opened my eyes again. For a moment I recalled nothing; then I remembered – and terror clutched at my heart. I pulled out my watch; it showed a quarter-past twelve. We began dinner at half-past eight. For more than three hours Molly had been in their hands.

I slipped my hand into my pocket and found that someone had taken my revolver. At that moment the lamp went out. There was no time to look for any weapon – no time for anything but to get to Molly at once.

And was there even time for that? As I raced through the orange grove towards the house the thought hammered at my brain. Was I too late?

I had no plan, except to get to Molly. What would happen then was beside the point.

A man sprang at me as I reached the door, and I hit him with all my weight. He went down like a log, and I felt better. Then I dashed into the passage, to pause for a moment in sheer amazement at the spectacle.

The braziers still poured forth their clouds of incense; the lamps were lit as in the afternoon. But the passage was crowded with natives.

They lay about on the floor in varying degrees of consciousness. Some were in a state of coma. Suddenly, quivering in the air, came the deep note of a drum. It was the signal for a wild outburst – drum madness: that strange phenomenon of Africa. Once again the deep note came quivering through the stifling air and died away.

Dodging between the writhing men, I rushed to the second door. It opened without difficulty – so that I stumbled forward on my face. The next moment half a dozen men had hurled themselves on me. I fought with the strength of despair, but it was useless. They got me up and held me – two of them to each arm, and what I saw almost snapped my reason.

Facing me were the three natives who had come to the *dahabeah* that night. They were on the other side of the pool – clad now in robes even more gorgeous than before. Behind them was the drum beater, rocking to and fro in ecstasy. Ranged on each side of them were other natives intoning a monotonous dirge that rose and fell in a strange cadence, culminating each time with the beat of the drum. At each beat I could feel the men holding me shiver in their excitement.

Below, in the pool, swirl after swirl of the black water showed that the crocodile was waiting for what was to come, as it knew – and I knew. For, standing on the platform, with her eyes still fixed on the leading native, was Molly.

I screamed her name. She took no notice, and once again I struggled desperately. If only I could get to her – pull her back – save her somehow! But they held me – there were six of them now – and when I shouted again one of them jammed my handkerchief into my mouth.

Suddenly the leader raised his hand, and Molly took another faltering step forward. One step more along the platform of death; one step nearer the end, where there would be only the pool below.

The drum increased; the voices rose...

Then it happened. Jim – Jim the superb, Jim the incomparable – was there on the other side of the pool. Jim with a jagged wound in his cheek, and his clothes in tatters, and such cold fury in his face as I have never seen in any man's before or since.

I heard the dull smash as he hit the drum beater, and then I went mad with the sheer tense excitement of it. With a great shout he seized the leader, and with one stupendous heave lifted him above his head. The others watched in stupefied silence, then with cries of fury closed in on him, only to stop as his voice rang out, speaking their own language.

"If anyone touches me, this man goes into the pool!"

He threw back his head and laughed, and the natives watched him, snarling and helpless.

"Go to her, Dick," he cried. The next instant Molly was safe – dazed, hypnotised, but still Molly. I dragged her off that damnable platform. As I hurried her to the door I looked back at Jim. The sweat was gleaming on his forehead; the strain of holding that full-grown native was taxing even his great strength. But once again he laughed that wonderful cheery laugh of his.

"To the boat, Dick. Good luck!"

In his heart of hearts that great-souled sportsman thought it was goodbye. Once – years after – he told me that he never thought he would see me again: the odds would be too great. For even now the natives were closing in on him, and suddenly one of them seized his arm.

"So be it," he roared, and with a mighty heave he threw his burden into the pool below.

I waited no longer. Taking advantage of the momentary stupefaction, Jim had vanished, and the next instant I was rushing Molly along the passage outside. With the cessation of the drum the natives there had become quieter, and none interfered with us. We reached the outer door and ran on towards the boat. Behind us I could hear a frenzied babel, but it seemed to come from the other side of the house. They were after Jim – the whole pack of them – and gradually the noise grew fainter and fainter. He was leading them away from us – just what Jim would do.

I darted on board to find the Captain and two of the crew standing there.

"Quick, sir," he cried, and I realised the engine was going. Already he was casting off, and I shouted to him to stop. Once Molly was safe I had to go back to help Jim.

I took her below and laid her on the berth in her cabin. Then I rushed on deck again to find that we were in mid-stream.

"Orders, sir," said the Captain. "Orders from the Englishman with the eyeglass."

I looked ashore: the bank was alive with lights. The shouting had died away: they were running mute, searching for him. Then suddenly I heard the most welcome sound I have ever heard in my life – Jim's laugh.

"Stop the old tub, Dick," came his voice. "I'm hanged if I'm going to swim to Cairo after you."

Then I saw him, saw his head reflected in the light from the bank. Half a minute later he swarmed up the side on a rope.

"Not a healthy spot, old Dick," he said with his hands on my shoulders. "Is the girl all right?"

"I think so," I answered, "thanks to you. But I feel dazed still. How did you get there?"

"All in good time," he laughed.

It was as we were going to the saloon that a sudden awful thought struck me.

"Jim," I muttered. "The Professor!"

Jim's face grew very stern.

"You needn't worry about the Professor," he remarked grimly, meaningly.

"You mean they've killed him?"

"Yes," he answered. "And I can think of no white man who more richly deserved to die."

As the boat chugged on through the soft Egyptian night, Jim filled in the gaps of the story.

"I didn't like it, as you know," he began, "right from the very start. Of course I hadn't an inkling when you left Cairo – but I was uneasy; and I made a few inquiries."

He paused and looked hard at me.

"Didn't it strike you, old man, that you got this *dahabeah* wonderfully promptly? That brute of a leader fixed it. He could fix most things when he put his mind to it, and this time he fixed it as the result of the most diabolical bargain with Professor Gainsford a man ever made.

"Mark you, I didn't find it out in Cairo – but I heard enough to send me off by train. I got out at Minieh, and then the game began. It's a good trek from the railway station, and with every mile the secrecy grew more profound.

"But I confirmed what I'd heard in Cairo. A great event was portending: you know how these things get about amongst the natives.

"Then you arrived, and I came on board. But not a soul was here. I sat down to wait, as I knew there was no danger till later. And then they caught me napping. A native came to the bank and told me he'd tell me everything: he'd just found out the truth. I scribbled that note, and followed him. He took me with great secrecy into the house, where someone promptly sandbagged me."

Jim laughed. "Me – at my age – sandbagged by a native! And when I came to I was trussed like a fowl, next to the skipper of this craft. It was he who told me the truth: Professor Gainsford wished to obtain some unique book of ritual belonging to this sect, and the native had agreed – you know at what price."

"What?" I roared. "You mean that he knew all along what was going to happen?"

Jim nodded gravely. "The native guaranteed silence; but, unfortunately for the Professor, the native mind is tortuous. The sacrifice of a white girl was his object, and he didn't mind what he promised to achieve it. Having, as he thought, achieved it when you all arrived, he changed his mind about the book of ritual. Which was unfortunate for the Professor."

He broke off suddenly and stared over my shoulder. Molly was standing in the door.

"Dick," she said, "I've had the most awful dream."

Jim and I looked at one another, and after a while he spoke.

"I'm afraid," he said gently, "that it wasn't a dream. Professor Gainsford is dead."

She swayed to a chair and sat down weakly.

"Dick!" she cried. "Why did we ever come here?" Then she stared at me with puzzled eyes. "But if it wasn't a dream – why, how did I see it?"

I went and knelt beside her.

"Leave that now, just for a while," I said gently. "Only try to remember that you are safe, thanks to Jim."

"Rot!" he cried cheerfully. "Though I admit it was touch and go till I found a sharp stone to cut my ropes. Now I think I'll leave you two for a bit."

And with that Jim turned on his heel and went forrard.

CHAPTER 10

An Experiment in Electricity

Little though we expected it at the time, there was a sequel to our Egyptian adventure. It took place in Berkeley Square of all places.

Jim kept to himself the possibility of such a thing while we were still in Egypt; and it was not till we were on board on our way home that he mentioned it to me. We had been watching the last belated sightseers hurrying across the gangway after a dash round Port Said, and now the first faint throb of the propellers heralded the final lap of the journey.

Slowly the gap between us and the shore widened; the native boats, with their chattering owners busily counting the proceeds, fell away. Suddenly Jim turned to me with a grin.

"This is the identical boat," he said, "in which I first left England."

"That deep thought seems to have made you very silent," I said with a laugh. "That's your first remark for half an hour."

He looked at me thoughtfully.

"Is Molly all right?" he asked.

"Molly?" I stared at him in some surprise. "Why – yes. I saw her going to her cabin with the parson's wife. What makes you ask?"

"Well, I don't mind telling you now what I didn't tell you in Cairo," said Jim quietly. "I've been distinctly uneasy these last two days."

"But what on earth about?" I asked.

"Our late friends at the Pool. I know that the place was empty when we went back; the birds had flown. But when you know as much about the native as I do, you will realise that that means nothing. Miss Tremayne escaped, and one of their chief scoundrels died in the process. A sect of that sort doesn't forgive such things. So when I received in Cairo a letter containing a typewritten threat I wasn't altogether surprised."

"But why didn't you tell me?" I cried.

He shrugged his shoulders.

"You couldn't have done anything, and I didn't want to run any risk of alarming you both."

"What was the threat?"

"Terse and to the point," laughed Jim. "It merely stated that, in view of what had happened, all our lives were forfeit, and would be claimed."

"How frightfully jolly!" I remarked. "Do you think it need be taken seriously?"

Once again he shrugged his shoulders.

"I take it a great deal less seriously now that we've left the country," he answered. "Undoubtedly the principal danger has passed, but I wouldn't say that we are out of the wood. It may have been merely an idle threat. The fact that nothing was tried on us in Cairo points that way. But you never know. Once you start monkeying with these fanatical sects you are asking for trouble.

"However," he went on, "there's nothing to be done. We can only wait and see if anything happens."

"It's possible," I said, "that the whole thing is merely designed to make us nervous, anticipating things which are never really coming."

"Possibly," Jim agreed. "If so, they succeeded quite well with me for forty-eight hours. Anyway, your girl is betraying no signs of nervousness. I'll go down below and pass the time of day with the purser, and incidentally fix up seats for tiffin."

The boat was fairly empty, and when Jim discovered that he knew the Captain it was agreed that we should sit at his table. A cheerful fellow, that skipper, and it was he who introduced us to Prince Selim.

"A charming man," he remarked, as Jim commented on the empty seat opposite him at lunch. "Fabulously wealthy, and almost more of an Englishman than an Egyptian. Has a large house in London, and spends most of his time there. I wonder you didn't meet him in Cairo."

The Prince came in at that moment. The Captain's remarks as to his appearance were quite justified. His clothes were faultless, and his face, save that it was a trifle darker, was that of a European. He was wonderfully good-looking, and when he smiled he showed perfect teeth. Moreover, he spoke English without a trace of accent. In fact, a charming man, with an astounding range of knowledge on all sorts of subjects and a fascinating way of imparting it.

Jim and I both took to him. He had travelled all over the world, and intelligently. Yet in spite of his roving propensities he was, the Captain said, an authority on old china, an electrical expert, and a wonderful violinist.

"I happen to know that much," said the skipper. "But from what I've seen of him, I shouldn't think it exhausts his repertoire."

Strangely enough, Molly didn't take to him.

"I don't know why it is, Dick," she said. "He's charming, he dances divinely, and he hasn't said a word that I could object to. But – I don't like him. It is probably all imagination, but there you are. And anyway it doesn't matter very much."

"The loss is entirely his," I laughed. "In all probability we shall never see him again after we land."

The voyage was most pleasant, and by the time Gibraltar hove in sight, Jim and his forebodings were forgotten. In four days we should be home, and life seemed very good.

I was in that comfortable frame of mind when I saw Jim coming along the deck towards me. The instant I saw his face I knew that something had happened. He glanced round to see that no one was within earshot; then he went straight to the point.

"I found this reposing on the pillow of my bunk an hour after we left Gib."

He held out a sheet of paper, containing one sentence, written with a typewriter:

Remember, all your lives are forfeit.

So much for the quiet life!

"How did it get there?" I asked at length.

"I know no more than you," he answered gravely. "I sent for our lascar at once" – Jim and I were sharing a cabin – "and frightened him. No good. I've made inquiries from one of the officers about the steerage passengers. He tells me definitely that there are no Arabs or Egyptians amongst them.

"How it got there," he continued after a moment, "is a trifle. A Scorp may have brought it off at Gib, and given it to one of the lascars; or, what is far more likely, it may have been handed to someone before we left Port Said with instructions to put it on my pillow when opportunity arose, and the bustle and excitement at Gib may have been the first chance. But, it doesn't matter how it got there: *why* is what concerns me. Is it just more stupid bluff – or is it something serious?"

"Why not ask Selim?" I said.

"Tell him the whole story," said Jim thoughtfully. "That's a good idea. Let's find him."

He was in the writing-room, and rose from his table on hearing we wanted his advice.

Without any exaggeration, but at the same time with some fullness, Jim told Prince Selim all about the Temple of the Sacred Crocodile.

"You actually threw this priest into the pool yourself?" he said, when we had finished.

"I did," said Jim grimly. "And if I'd had time I'd have thrown the rest. The point, Prince, is this. Are those letters bluff or not?"

"Most emphatically not," answered the Prince promptly. "You may take it from me that you only encountered the fringe of that sect. You have killed a high priest – and that they will never forgive. Whether or not they will be able to carry out their purpose in England is a different matter; they will assuredly try."

"What – to kill the lot of us?" said Jim.

"Certainly," said the Prince calmly. "And deeply as I regret to say so, my friend, I wouldn't be at all surprised if they succeeded."

Jim's jaw came out.

"We'll see about that," he remarked quietly. "Meantime, Prince, what do you suggest?"

"Nothing," he answered. "They will find you wherever you hide yourselves; then it will be you or them."

"Hide!" Jim stared at him in amazement. "My dear fellow, why in the name of fortune should we hide ourselves?"

The Prince waved a deprecating hand.

"Possibly I expressed myself a little infelicitously," he murmured. "Your courage is beyond dispute. But, for all that – "

"You can take it from me, Prince," said Jim quietly, "that I don't propose to go into seclusion. But Miss Tremayne is different. If you think her life is in danger we had better take steps. Naturally, she knows nothing of these letters, and one doesn't want to alarm her."

"Precisely," said the Prince, as we watched him a little anxiously.

"I will tell you what I suggest," he said at length. "If you become aware that they are after you, come and see me. I will give you my address, and possibly I may be of assistance. But we cannot evolve any scheme now. Let us leave it until we have an idea. Then – well, three heads are better than two."

"That's sporting of you, Prince," said Jim. "We accept with gratitude."

"Certainly," I agreed. "And you don't think there is any need to alarm Miss Tremayne, or take any special precautions?"

"I do not," said Prince Selim. "If the attempt is made, I feel certain it will be in London."

A moment or two later he rose and left us.

It was just a week after we reached London that the blow fell – and in London itself, in a house in the middle of Mayfair, it seemed more amazing than anything that had happened by the Nile. It appeared even at the time to be unreal and incredible.

I had been out all the afternoon shopping with Molly. We were going to a theatre that night, and I had returned to my club to dress. I found Jim waiting for me in a state of unconcealed impatience.

"I thought you were never coming, Dick," he cried. "Take me where we can talk."

I led the way to a small empty card-room.

"You know I gave Selim my address?" he began. "An hour ago I was told that someone wanted me on the telephone. It was the Prince."

Jim stared at me gravely.

"It's evidently no leg-pull, Dick."

"What did he say?" I asked.

"'Thank Heaven you're still alive.' He didn't beat about the bush at all, but came straight to the point. 'You're in the most deadly peril,' he said. 'I've just received information which you should know at once. It is too long to tell you over the telephone, even if I dared.' So I arranged that you and I are to go round to his house this evening at nine. The time is important, as he will then arrange that his Arab butler is out. That little precaution is for *his* benefit. He told me it would be signing his own death sentence if it were known he was warning us. He will then tell us what he has found out, and it will be up to us after that.

"I asked about Molly. She is perfectly safe for the next twelve hours. He further asked if we would both be good enough to preserve absolute silence as to where we were going. That – also for his sake.

"You see, he made no bones about the fact that he is running a grave risk, and wanting it minimised. That is quite understandable, because there's really no call on the fellow to do anything at all."

"None whatever," I agreed. "I must ring up Molly at once, and tell her I can't go tonight. After that you'd better have early dinner with me."

All through that meal we discussed what this danger could be that threatened us. The whole thing seemed so fantastic. Just as we had advanced the sixth wild guess, I saw one of the page-boys coming towards me.

"There's a black man to see you, sir, in the hall."

I glanced at Jim; then followed the boy.

"This man, sir," began the porter; then stared round foolishly, for the hall was empty.

"Hey! boy – where's that Arab?" he said.

But the page-boy didn't know, and the sergeant outside didn't know. They were positive that an Arab had entered the club, to inquire for me, but – They were still arguing about it when Jim and I were ready to go.

"They're on to us, Dick," he said gravely. "That man merely came round to find out if you were in. It's only fair to Selim to throw any possible watchers off the scent if we can. Let us, therefore, announce in a loud tone outside that we are going to Hampstead. Then we can double back in case we're being followed."

He gave an address in Eton Avenue, while I looked round. Not a soul was in sight – certainly no other vehicle, but we were taking no chances. In Oxford Street we gave the driver the real address we wanted in Berkeley Square. Even then we didn't give him the number: we intended to walk the last few yards.

"Have you a gun?" said Jim suddenly.

"I haven't," I answered. "But we shan't want one tonight."

He laughed shortly. "No – I suppose not. But I don't sort of feel dressed without. I wonder what this is going to develop into."

"We shall know very soon," I said. "It's five to nine, and here is Berkeley Square."

The door was opened by the Prince himself, and he immediately shut it again behind us.

"Follow me, please, gentlemen. There is not a moment to be lost."

He led the way through the hall to a heavy green-baize door at the farther end. Down two flights of steps we hurried, till another door barred our progress. The Prince produced a key, and the next moment an exclamation of wonder broke from both our lips as we saw into the room beyond. For a while I forgot the real object of our visit in my amazement.

It was a big room divided by an ornamental grille. There was an opening in the centre, and the grille itself hardly obstructed one's view at all. But it was the beauty of the furniture and the wonderful lighting effect that riveted my attention: it seemed like a room out of a fairy story.

The general design was Oriental. Luxurious divans: marvellous Persian rugs: small inlaid tables of gold and silver: water trickling through the leaves of a great mass of tropical flowers: and over everything the soft glow of hidden lights. The Prince smiled faintly.

"A room on which I have expended a good deal of time and money," he remarked. "The general effect is, I think, not unpleasing. I use it a lot when I am in London. Some of the things are unique. For instance, that chair in which you are sitting, Mr Leyton, was used by the Doges of Venice. Now put your arms along the sides as you would when sitting comfortably. By the way, Maitland, there's a head through there that will interest you. A record specimen, I'm told."

"That's comfortable now," I said as Jim strolled into the other half of the room.

"Well, all I do," said the Prince, "is to turn this little lever behind your head, and there you are."

"Well!" I exclaimed. "That's neat."

Two curved pieces of metal, which were normally parallel to the arms and quite unnoticeable, turned inwards through a right angle and pressed lightly on my wrists. But though the pressure was negligible, it was effective. The curve of the metal held my hands: my elbows were hard against the back of the chair. I could not reach the lever at the back of the chair. I was a prisoner.

"That's extraordinarily neat, Prince," I repeated. "So absurdly simple, too."

At that moment there came a faint clang: the opening through which Jim passed had shut.

"Absurdly simple, indeed," agreed the Prince pleasantly. "But then, my friend – so are you."

The silence was absolute. Jim swung round, and shook the grille. It refused to budge.

"Is this a game, Prince?" he asked quietly.

"I don't know whether you will find it so, Mr Maitland. I think so, but you may not."

"So it was a trap, was it?" Jim said. "I confess I'm a little in the dark, but doubtless I shall not remain so for long."

"You will not," agreed the other. "In fact, I propose to enlighten you now. When you first went into that half of the room, it was just a normal room. Now, I regret to state, things are rather different."

He stretched himself out in an easy-chair and lit a cigarette.

"You may happen to have heard, Mr Maitland, that I am an expert on electricity. This last week I have been busy on an electrifying scheme. Having been cheated of my excitement at the Pool of the Sacred Crocodile, I am sure you will agree that you owe me some reparation."

"So you were there!" said Jim slowly.

"Certainly I was there," answered the Prince. "And though I was quite amused, the evening had not quite the same zest as if the charming Molly had gone into the pool."

"You blackguard," I roared, struggling.

"Please don't let any thought of her mar your enjoyment, Mr Leyton," the Prince murmured. "I will look after her with great pleasure when you are unable to."

He turned once again to Jim, who had slipped his hand into his pocket.

"Take it out, and have a chat," said the Prince, with a faint smile.

"Confound it!" cried Jim. "What's the matter with the gun? Who is tugging at my pocket?"

He swung round with his fists clenched, and an amazed look on his face. He was alone; yet I could see the pocket that contained his revolver being dragged from him, as if by an invisible hand.

"Electricity," the Prince went on affably.

Just then Jim managed to extricate his revolver. The Egyptian leant forward and pressed a button.

It looked as if the revolver was wrenched from Jim's hand. It crashed at his feet, while he stared at it bewildered. It was resting on two small pillars which stuck up a few inches from the floor, and though he tugged at it with all his great strength, it stayed there.

Once again the Prince smiled faintly. "Magnetism, Maitland," he murmured.

I saw sweat gleaming on Jim's forehead.

"What's all this leading to?" he said a little hoarsely, staring at the Egyptian.

"What I told you – an evening's amusement."

Suddenly Jim lost his temper. He sprang at the gate and shook it wildly, only to give a shout of pain and jump back again.

"A severe electric shock," said the Prince genially. "Not enough to do real harm, but enough to prove to you that I am not bluffing. You know the principles of electricity, don't you?"

The Prince lit another cigarette, and lay back luxuriously in his chair.

"You remember, doubtless, the method of getting a shock by holding two terminals. That is what happened a moment ago, except that you were standing on one terminal, and holding the other."

"Suppose you quit fooling," said Jim grimly.

"Certainly," said the Prince. "Since I last saw you I have fixed scores of similar terminals all over your half of the room. For instance – the chair just behind you. There are two there. You might sit for quite a time, then some chance movement might make the connection. Then you'd get another shock."

"Am I to understand," snarled Jim, "that you propose to keep me hopping round having shocks?"

He took a step towards the grille, to stop abruptly at the Prince's shout of warning.

"Not yet! I couldn't bear to lose you so soon."

"What do you mean?" said Jim.

"When you shook the gate before only one-fiftieth of the current was switched on. But now it's all on. You would be electrocuted far too soon. I should have had no fun at all."

The Prince lay back as if appalled at such a narrow escape, and Jim stood very still.

"They're all over the room," he explained. "At this very moment you may be within an inch of death. I mean that. If you moved your right foot, you might complete the circuit. On the other hand, you may not be within a yard of it. That's the game. Just like hunt the thimble. Sometimes as you move about the room you'll be warm, and sometimes you'll be cold – and I wait and watch. It may last a minute; it may be an hour or more. Some of the death spots I know; some I do not. They were put in by another. That makes it more exciting."

He pressed a button, and an Arab came in with champagne and caviare sandwiches, and departed noiselessly. Still Jim stood motionless, staring at the Prince. Was it bluff or not? That was the thought in both our minds.

"You can, of course, continue standing exactly where you are with perfect impunity," continued the Prince suavely. "As a matter of fact, as this is my first experiment, I am quite interested in the psychology of the thing. How long will you go on standing there? Four hours – five? The night is yet young. But sooner or later, my dear Maitland, you will have to move. Sleep will overcome you, and that will be dangerous for you, Maitland. But interesting for me."

"What's your object in doing this?" said Jim slowly, after a long pause.

"Amusement principally – and revenge. How dared you, you miserable Englishman, profane our temple and put the authorities on us?"

With his teeth bared like a wolf's, the Egyptian rose and approached the grille. He stood there snarling, and Jim yawned.

"You murdered a man," went on the Prince, and his voice was shaking with rage, "a man who had forgotten more of the mysteries of life than you and all your miserable countrymen will ever know. The penalty for that is death, as I told you."

"So you wrote those notes!" said Jim in a bored voice. "You wretched little Dago."

In a frenzy the Egyptian shook both his fists.

"Yes, it was I," he screamed. "And it was I who went round to your club this evening, and heard you order the car to go to Hampstead, and bluffed you all through. It was considerate of you, Maitland, to tell the taxi-driver that. There are excellent places on the tube line out there where your bodies can be found – electrocuted. And as I've told you" – he turned to me – "I will look after Molly."

With a great effort he recovered himself and sat down again. Motionless as a statue, Jim still stood there, and his eyes never left the Prince's face.

I sat watching him helplessly. I knew that this was not bluff, and that Jim never stood in such deadly peril as at that moment. Sooner or later he *must* move, and risk sudden death. But the hand that held and lit his cigarette was steady as a rock.

He smoked it through, while the Egyptian watched him as a cat watches a mouse. It couldn't go on, we all knew that; and as Jim flung the end away the Prince approached the grille. On his face was a horrible look of anticipation; his sinewy hands were clenched tight.

"Well, old Dick," said Jim steadily, "this appears to be the end of a sporting course. I refuse to stand here any more for the amusement of that nigger. So I propose to sit down. And in case I sit the wrong way – goodbye."

He turned and lounged towards the big chair.

"A poor chair this, Selim," said Jim mildly – and then it happened. Jim gave one convulsive leap and slithered to the floor, where he lay rigid and stiff. For a moment I was stunned; for a moment I forgot that it was my fate, too. I could only grasp that Jim was dead. There was madness in the eyes of Prince Selim, as he turned on me.

"Your turn next," he snarled, "but first we will remove the body."

He pressed over a switch on the wall, and a great blue spark stabbed the air. Then he went to the central gate and pulled it back.

"Not much sport that time," he remarked. "Too quick. But, anyway, my dear Leyton, you will now know one place to avoid."

"Which is more than you do!" came a terrible voice, and the Prince screamed. Jim's hands were round his throat, and Jim's merciless eyes were boring into his brain.

"You're not the only person who can bluff, Selim," he shouted.

The grip tightened, and the Egyptian struggled madly to free himself, until quite suddenly he grew limp, and Jim flung him into the chair, where he lay sprawling. Then, picking up his revolver, he came towards me.

"Touch and go that time, Dick," he said, as with a strained look in his eyes he set me free.

"I thought you were done, old man," I said hoarsely. "When you doubled up like that – " I broke off as Jim crossed to the switch.

"I knew he wasn't bluffing," he said. "I saw that in his eyes. Now we'll see how he likes it."

There came another vivid spark, and with a loud clang the gate closed in the grille, while the Egyptian still sprawled unconscious in the chair.

"So I took the only possible way as it seemed to me. If it failed – I died, and by the mercy of Allah it didn't. Great Heavens! Look!"

His hand gripped my arm, and I swung round just in time to see the Prince crash forward and lie still.

"No," repeated Jim, and his hand shook a little, "it wasn't bluff."

So I come to the finish. Jim wasn't our best man after all, for we had a double wedding.

For he found her – the girl he had last seen in the hotel at Tampico. Fate gave the wheel a kindly twist, and the harbour for which, in his heart of hearts, Jim had long been steering, hove in sight.

It happened quite suddenly, one afternoon. At first I could hardly believe my eyes; but after a moment or two I knew that it was no mistake: the girl talking to Molly was Jim's girl.

It was in a hat shop where Molly had taken me. It appeared that she often came to this shop, which was run by a lady who had built up the business herself. She had struggled through a bad time and now had made good. Sheila Bernie was her name, and from the corner to which I had retired I saw her come out from an inner sanctum and greet Molly. And Sheila Bernie was the girl I had known as Sheila Blair – wife of Raymond Blair, who lay buried in Tampico.

Molly called me up to introduce me, and for a moment the girl stared at me with a puzzled frown.

"Surely," she said, "we have met somewhere?"

I bowed and took her hand.

"Tampico," I said. "In the South Seas."

I heard her catch her breath, and then I went on.

"Mr Maitland and I landed in London about a month ago."

I knew that Molly was looking from one to the other of us, but even when the girl went on, with her head thrown back in that queer little way that I remembered so well, Molly said nothing. She is one of those rare people who knows when to speak and when not.

"Will you tell Mr Maitland," she said quietly, "that I made a mistake which I have never ceased regretting. I can quite understand that he will find it impossible to forgive me, but I had no method of communicating with him."

"I will certainly tell him," I assured her. "But is there any reason, Mrs Blair, why you shouldn't tell him yourself?"

For a moment she hesitated.

Then: "I am here every day from nine till five."

She turned to Molly, but Molly's interest in hats seemed to have waned. Tea was her sole thought; and she would come back when she had more time. So tea it was, and at tea came questions.

"Tell me everything, Dick. Why did you call her Mrs Blair? I've known her now for two years, and stayed with her down in her little bungalow in Sussex. She's never mentioned that she was married."

"Her husband died some years ago," I said. "It's an amazing coincidence, running into her this afternoon. I think Jim had given up hope of ever seeing her again."

Then I told her the story.

"In your life, Molly," I said, "you've probably never come across such a case, and don't know what a real drunkard is. He isn't a man at all. Blair wasn't."

"And that was Sheila's husband!"

I nodded. "Jim might have taken Blair to the hotel as he was, and then waited for the inevitable end. But he didn't: he turned him into something comparatively normal. That seemed to Jim the only way of playing the game. But you could hardly expect the girl to understand that.

"What Blair said to her I don't know. I suppose she found him peculiar and changed – I suppose he tried to make some pitiful excuse. At any rate she found out what Jim had done, and she didn't know why. She thought he had deliberately made her husband drunk.

"I suppose she knew Jim was in love with her, and she thought he hoped to blacken her husband in her eyes. So she called Jim a cur, and told him she never wished to see him again. Jim wouldn't let MacAndrew or me explain. He just stood there until she'd finished – and at the top of the stairs stood her husband. One could almost hear him saying, 'Don't give me away.' And Jim didn't."

"That was big, Dick," said Molly, and her eyes were shining. "She knows now, anyway."

"Yes," I answered. "During the six months of her husband's life she must have seen him sober fairly often. And maybe MacAndrew told her, later."

"So it's all come right after all," cried Molly. "You'll tell Jim, and – "

"I shall tell Jim," I answered. "But he's a queer proud sort of blighter, and – "

"You don't mean to say he'll be such an ass as to stick in his toes and jib?"

"Dash it all!" I said rather feebly. "You must admit that it's galling to be abused like a pickpocket for doing one of the whitest things a man could possibly have done."

"That was years ago. He ought to have forgotten all about it by this time."

"Well, he hasn't," I said. "Besides, how do you know that she is in love with him?"

"Because I saw her face when you mentioned his name."

"You weren't looking at her."

"My good man," said Molly kindly, "don't expose your ignorance too much. These things are beyond you. I have decided that Jim and Sheila Bernie – or Blair, whichever you prefer – are to be married on the same day as you and I. You will tell him where she is, and, if necessary, conduct him there tomorrow morning. You will then leave them alone, and engage a table for four at the Ritz for lunch."

"Bismillah!" I murmured. "Everything shall be as you say."

Up to a point, it was. I dined with Jim that night at my club, and told him.

"I've some wonderful news for you, old man. Who do you think I saw this afternoon?"

He sat very still staring at me.

"You've seen her, Dick?" he said at length. "Tell me – how does she look?"

"You'll see for yourself, tomorrow morning." For the life of me I couldn't keep my voice quite steady. "You're to go round and bring her to lunch with us at the Ritz. It's all fixed up. You're to tell her to shut up her shop for the remainder of the day."

He laid his hand on my shoulder as we strolled out of the dining-room.

"Methinks I see the work of Molly in that arrangement, Dick. Bless both your hearts!"

And so we fell to yarning till the reproachful eye of the waiter woke us to the fact that the last member had left half an hour ago. They were good years to look back on, those we had spent together, and now he, as well as I, had the wonderful years to look forward to. Jim came with me to the door, and for a few moments we stood there.

"Fine weather, old Dick; fine weather in front. And happy days behind. Surely the world is good."

SAPPER

The Black Gang

Although the First World War is over, it seems that the hostilities are not, and when Captain Hugh 'Bulldog' Drummond discovers that a stint of bribery and blackmail is undermining England's democratic tradition, he forms the Black Gang, bent on tracking down the perpetrators of such plots. They set a trap to lure the criminal mastermind behind these subversive attacks to England, and all is going to plan until Bulldog Drummond accepts an invitation to tea at the Ritz with a charming American clergyman and his dowdy daughter.

Bulldog Drummond

'Demobilised officer, finding peace incredibly tedious, would welcome diversion. Legitimate, if possible; but crime, if of a comparatively humorous description, no objection. Excitement essential... Reply at once Box X10.'

Hungry for adventure following the First World War, Captain Hugh 'Bulldog' Drummond begins a career as the invincible protectorate of his country. His first reply comes from a beautiful young woman, who sends him racing off to investigate what at first looks like blackmail but turns out to be far more complicated and dangerous. The rescue of a kidnapped millionaire, found with his thumbs horribly mangled, leads Drummond to the discovery of a political conspiracy of awesome scope and villainy, masterminded by the ruthless Carl Peterson.

SAPPER

BULLDOG DRUMMOND AT BAY

While Hugh 'Bulldog' Drummond is staying in an old cottage for a peaceful few days duck-shooting, he is disturbed one night by the sound of men shouting, followed by a large stone that comes crashing through the window. When he goes outside to investigate, he finds a patch of blood in the road, and is questioned by two men who tell him that they are chasing a lunatic who has escaped from the nearby asylum. Drummond plays dumb, but is determined to investigate in his inimitable style when he discovers a cryptic message.

THE FEMALE OF THE SPECIES

Bulldog Drummond has slain his arch-enemy, Carl Peterson, but Peterson's mistress lives on and is intent on revenge. Drummond's wife vanishes, followed by a series of vicious traps set by a malicious adversary, which lead to a hair-raising chase across England, to a sinister house and a fantastic torture-chamber modelled on Stonehenge, with its legend of human sacrifice.

S A P P E R

The Final Count

When Robin Gaunt, inventor of a terrifyingly powerful weapon of chemical warfare, goes missing, the police suspect that he has 'sold out' to the other side. But Bulldog Drummond is convinced of his innocence, and can think of only one man brutal enough to use the weapon to hold the world to ransom. Drummond receives an invitation to a sumptuous dinner-dance aboard an airship that is to mark the beginning of his final battle for triumph.

The Return of Bulldog Drummond

While staying as a guest at Merridale Hall, Captain Hugh 'Bulldog' Drummond's peaceful repose is disturbed by a frantic young man who comes dashing into the house, trembling and begging for help. When two warders arrive, asking for a man named Morris – a notorious murderer who has escaped from Dartmoor – Drummond assures them that they are chasing the wrong man. In which case, who on earth is this terrified youngster?

19721527R00093

Printed in Great Britain
by Amazon